MW01114147

THE TECH SUPERHEROES

SIYA SHARMA
SANVI JAIN

The Tech Superheroes

ISBN 978-1-66785-821-0
eBook ISBN 978-1-66785-822-7

Dedicated to our families

TABLE OF CONTENTS

CHAPTER ONE:

MISSION TECH

It was early on a hot summer morning in the middle of August in Tampa, Florida. The year was 2045. The sun was starting to warm up the air as the thirteen-year-old triplets hurriedly walked to their new job. Their parents had left for a business trip when they were five and never returned. They had left some money and a caretaker, but after a few months, the caretaker left. The kids had waited and waited until they finally realized they had to support themselves. They left school and started looking for jobs.

"I am so glad we got this job," Kayla said. "It's been really hard to find jobs since we have been fired so many times."

"Yeah, so far, we have been fired from the police station, science company, art store, grocery store, financial department …" Ash went on.

All three siblings were tall and tanned, with dark brown eyes and short brown hair. Ash was the shortest of the three and had slightly lighter skin than her sister, Kayla. "But I am excited to start our new job. We're supposed to earn a lot of money here."

"Yup," Kayla said to her older sister. "I am so excited to start. More excited than you, Ash."

Ash was only five hours older than Kayla.

"You aren't," Ash said.

"I am," Kayla said.

"Aren't."

"Am."

"Aren't!"

"Am!"

"Can you guys stop now?" Nick looked more like Ash than Kayla. He was three hours older than Ash and took his responsibilities seriously as the three's eldest.

"All right," Ash said, and there was silence for a while.

"The interview didn't go well," Nick said, breaking the silence. "I wonder why they even hired us. I mean, they hired us even after finding out how many jobs we have gotten fired from!"

"Yeah, and we kept forgetting what to say, and we kept looking confused for whatever the interviewing person said," Kayla added, wincing.

"And no offense Kayla, but you were making too many jokes and talking like a child," Ash informed her.

"Hey! At least I said something! You and Nick kept waiting before you said anything! Like you were making the biggest decision of your life!"

"Well, excuse us if we actually cared about what we said!" Nick said.

"Guys!" Ash said. Let's stop fighting and get back to the topic! At least we got hired, even if the interview did go terribly wrong!"

"I guess we have to be nineteen to work here," Nick agreed. "Do you think that we should tell them?"

"Of course not!" Kayla exclaimed. "This job sounds really fun. Why would we blow our covers? We got here by chance! We can't let it go!"

"Seriously, you don't have to get so mad!" Nick exclaimed. "I was just asking!"

"Well, I hope our new boss trusts the video we sent in," Ash said.

"If she didn't trust it, why would she give us the job?" Kayla asked.

The first round of the hiring process was sending in a video profile about themselves, which led them to be able to do a video interview. The company insisted on a video interview for the second round of interviews because they didn't want applicants to know the location of the secret science agency, Mission Tech.

Nick, Kayla, and Ash were on their way to their first day on the job now.

"Are we there yet?" Ash asked.

"Well, the Glic-Map shows us that we are literally standing on top of Mission Tech, but we are obviously not," Nick said. He looked around. "Yup, we aren't."

Ash looked over Nick's shoulder at the directions on the Glic-Map's holographic screen. "Yup, Nick is right. The map says that we are actually standing on top of Mission Tech."

"Maybe it's invisible!" Kayla suggested excitedly.

"How could it be invisible?" Nick asked. "We can't feel it anywhere!"

"Maybe it's transparent," Kayla tried again, still excited.

Ash replied, "It would be way too hard to make so—"

"Ahhhhhhhhh!" they screamed as the ground beneath them suddenly opened up, and they plummeted into a dark hole before landing abruptly.

"Ow," Ash moaned, face flat on the sandy, rocky ground.

Nick helped her get up.

"Where are we?" Kayla asked, dusting off her clothes.

"I have no idea," Nick replied, looking around.

They had landed in a dark, rocky cave with a gray tunnel, the only exit since the hole they had fallen through was gone as if a trap door had closed. The floor was brownstone, but there was some sand on it. There were many overlapping footprints around the tunnel, and the ground felt like many people had been on it. The air was warm and smelled damp. There were footprints everywhere, but most of them led to one place. There, was dust everywhere and worn-out walls and floors. Glowing lanterns on the sides of the cave allowed them to see.

"I know!" Kayla exclaimed. "We are in a secret passage!"

"Well, I'm pretty sure that this is Mission Tech," Ash said, "as the Glic-Map says, this is the exact location where Mission Tech is supposed to be. Plus, in the email the CEO sent us, she said it would be pretty secure, and there would be a secret passage we would have to follow to reach her office. So, like she said in the email, let's follow the secret passage and meet her."

"Why would Mission Tech be in a cave?" Nick asked.

"I don't know," Kayla said. "I guess we'll have to find out."

They started to walk in the tunnel, following the footprints. After a million hours, they found themselves standing a few feet from the end of the passage.

"Now what?" Kayla asked.

"Well, there is a slide over there," Ash replied, pointing to a green tube slide coming out of the wall. "We probably just have to slide down."

"Who wants to go first?" Nick asked.

"Me!" Kayla and Ash said at the same time.

"Um, Kayla, you can go first," Ash suggested.

"Yay!" Kayla exclaimed, pumping her fists in the air. "Thaaaaaanks," she called as she slid out of sight. Ash followed, and Nick went last. A minute later, the slide ended in a room with many doors. Each door had three names on it, indicating whose room was whose.

"That was fun!" Kayla exclaimed as she walked toward the doors.

"I know!" Ash agreed, moving to stand next to her. "I want to go on it again!"

"Yeah!" Kayla said happily. "I mean, like, it w—"

"Guys, focus!" Nick interrupted.

"Oops, sorry," Ash said.

Kayla looked past Nick. "Wow! There are a lot of doors!"

"I know," Nick agreed. "Anyway, which door should we go through? We are supposed to meet the C.E.O., Pegasus."

"It would be so weird if she were Pegasus Bliesti," Ash said.

"She is," Kayla said significantly. "I mean, how many people in the world have a name like 'Pegasus'? That's like the name of the Greek flying horse or something."

"Yeah, right!" Nick scoffed. "The richest person in the country is our boss."

"I'm just saying," Kayla said with a shrug.

"So, let's think, which door?" Ash asked.

"Ummmm," Nick said, scratching his forehead.

"How about the third door?" Kayla suggested. "It has Pegasus written on it."

"Sure!" Ash exclaimed. "Great eye, Kayla!"

They walked through the third door. In the corner of the room was a long gray stone staircase. The triplets began to walk up the stairs with a silent shrug. At the top of it was a white door.

"Should we go through this door?" Nick asked.

"Why not?" Ash shrugged.

"I suppose," Nick said.

He opened the door. As soon as he did, the room flooded with light. Another staircase led up, and they exchanged silent glances again and headed up. At the top, they walked along a hallway until it dead-ended at the door with the letters C.E.O. on a brass nameplate.

Nick opened the door. Once again, the light immediately filled the vast room. They felt as if they could hear a choir singing. Despite the bright light, they could barely see the other side; the room was large. The walls were the perfect shade of gold, and a soft, plush white carpet was on the floor. The room had to be huge to hold the wide variety of items the triplets could see: Portraits of Pegasus Bliesti, a marble desk, a huge kitchen, an immense hallway with lots of doors, a couch, many chairs, a giant safe, computers, Glic-Screens, and filing cabinets took up much of the space. Detective supplies, like a magnifying glass, tweezers, plastic bags for evidence, and so on were also visible. The room was rectangular and had a hallway in the middle. On their right was the kitchen, and on the left was the executive desk. There was a small pink fluffy carpet underneath the desk.

The Glic-Screen looked like a watch but had a large black button in the middle. Pressing the button on the phone-like device, worn on the wrist, caused a holographic screen to appear.

"OMG!" Ash squealed. "This place is amazing! I have never seen anything like it!"

"This is awesome," Kayla said.

Nick couldn't say anything. He just stared in awe.

"Is this an office or a royal palace?" Ash asked.

"I have no idea!" Kayla exclaimed. "But it's awesome!"

"Guys!" Nick yelled from the kitchen. "This place has an ice cream bar!"

Kayla and Ash rushed over.

"Wow!" Ash exclaimed.

Kayla, Ash, and Nick took out helpings and helpings of the ice cream.

"Howdy," said a southern accent behind them.

"AAAAHHHH!" Nick, Ash, and Kayla screamed as they turned around.

"Is that who I think it is?" Kayla asked.

"Dude, this is absolutely who you think it is," Ash said, her eyes widening with surprise.

"Seriously, this is so cool," Nick said.

"Uh-huh," Kayla and Ash said.

"Howdy," the woman said again. "Did I introduce myself?"

CHAPTER TWO:

MEETING THE C.E.O.

"My name is Pegasus Bliesti," the woman said, standing up straighter. She was wearing a white dress with pink flowers and had honey skin. She had a bright smile, but it didn't reach her cold, gray eyes. "I am the CEO of this company."

"I knew it!" Kayla said. "I told you she was Pegasus Bliesti, like, ten minutes ago!"

"We know," Ash groaned.

"Howdy," Pegasus said for the second time, putting her hand out.

"I can't believe I am actually meeting Pegasus Bilesti!" Kayla said.

Kayla grabbed Pegasus's hand and shook it really, really hard.

"Kayla, stop; you are hurting her," Nick whispered.

"Oh, sorry," Kayla apologized.

Ash rolled her eyes.

"Let's go to my desk, shall we?" Pegasus asked politely. "I think that would be more appropriate for this meeting."

"Yeah, I agree," Ash said.

They walked over to Pegasus's desk. There were three chairs on one side and one chair on the other side. They sat down.

"So, welcome to this company, Nicholas, Ashley, and McKayla Hall," Pegasus said. "How are you today?"

"Great!" Nick exclaimed.

"Yup," Kayla agreed. "But if you don't mind, we prefer our nicknames."

"Yeah," Ash said. "The person you called Nicholas is Nick, I'm Ash, and my sister here is Kayla. We don't like to be called by our full names."

"Okay, sure," Pegasus said. "Are you excited to start your first day here at Mission Tech?"

"Uh-huh," Nick said.

"As you should know, this is not just a technology company; this place also works on some critical missions," Pegasus informed them. "You will not only be learning technology but also how to be a spy and a detective."

"Yup, we know," Kayla said.

"Good," Pegasus continued. "Now, I would like to tell you that I know nearly everything about y'all. Since we work on mission-critical projects, we always run detailed background checks on everyone we hire."

Nick, Ash, and Kayla's eyes widened, and there was fear in their eyes.

"So," Pegasus continued, "I know that y'all are just thirteen years old. Your trainers also know everything about you, so there is no need to worry. We will still allow you to work here at Mission Tech."

"Um, why?" Ash asked. "Don't you only hire people that are at least sixteen years old?"

"Yeah," Nick agreed. "We're three years too young."

"No," Pegasus said. "Everyone that I have hired is special. I don't hire people based on age, only their talents and abilities."

"Um, what talents and abilities do we have that made you want to hire us?" Ash asked.

"You'll figure out soon enough," Pegasus said with a smile.

"Is it okay if we wear informal clothes?" Kayla asked. "Because we don't really have formal clothes."

"Don't worry," Pegasus reassured them. "Everyone here wears what they like. Do you think a CEO would dress the way I do? Probably not."

"Okay, good," Ash said.

"Now, you guys must be wondering why we hired you," Pegasus said. "There is an evil man on the loose named Dark King. He is trying to take over the world. We need you to help stop him."

"But we are only thirteen," Nick said, confused.

"Sometimes children are smarter than adults at specific things," Pegasus said with a smile. "Now, how about y'all go and check out your office before you start training? A secret passage in my office has direct slide access to all Mission Tech offices. Search for your names, and you can slide down directly to your office."

"Uh, okay," Ash said.

"Nice to meet y'all," she said.

"Nice to meet you too," Nick said.

"Well, that was easy," Kayla said as they left. They walked into the hallway, which led them to a blue room with more than a hundred vertical, clear-glass tubes that looked like cylinder elevators. Three people could fit inside each one, and they all had names on them.

"Yeah, Pegasus was so cool and nice and awesome!" Ash exclaimed, looking around the room. "Whoa!"

Kayla glanced around in surprise, and so did Nick.

"Wow, this is amazing!" Nick agreed.

"I agree," Kayla said. "What about you, Nick?"

"Huh?" Nick asked, turning toward Kayla. "About what?"

"About Pegasus!" She reminded him.

"I don't like her," Nick said. "There is something about her that I can't put my finger on. She is not how I expected her to be. For some reason, I find her to be untrustworthy and dangerous. And pretty arrogant."

"Are you crazy?!" Ash exclaimed. "I thought she was amazing!

"Everyone has different opinions," Kayla said with a shrug.

"Yeah," Nick agreed. "Everyone does."

"So, which one?" Ash asked.

"Which one of what?" Kayla asked.

Ash slapped her forehead. "I mean, which tube!"

Kayla looked around the room. "Ohhhhhhhh!"

"Seriously?" Ash asked, raising her eyebrow.

"Guys!" Nick said. "Focus!"

"I can see our names on the one all the way at the back of the room," Kayla said.

"There you go," Nick said.

They walked to the back, stepped into their tube, and then, like an elevator, it whooshed down.

CHAPTER THREE:
BILLY BELIMA

"AHHH!" they all screamed as they sped along the tube before landing in a vast hallway.

"That was fun!" Kayla and Ash exclaimed.

"Yeah," Nick agreed as they got out of the glass cylinder.

"Whoa, where are we?" Nick asked, looking around.

The large hallway where the tube had stopped was turquoise in color and had four brown doors leading out from it. One said Office, while the second one said Training Room. The third one said Sports Room and the last one said Bedroom. The three looked at each other before walking to the door labeled Training Room. The large white room was divided up into smaller spaces by glass partitions. Each small room had a desk, a chair, an emergency pole, and cabinets.

"It's nice, right?" a short, round man with a British accent, black curly hair, dark brown skin, and blue eyes asked.

"Ahhhh!" Nick, Ash, and Kayla screamed. They turned around, and Kayla giggled at the sight of the man wearing a blue shirt, blue pants, and blue sneakers. On his head was a hair band adorned with a huge blue pom-pom.

"Sorry for scaring you," the man apologized, oblivious to their laughter.

"It's all right," Ash said.

"Kayla, stop laughing," Nick hissed into Kayla's ear.

"Sorry, he has such weird clothes!" Kayla whispered back.

"McKayla Hall!" Nick hissed back.

"Sorry, Saint Nicholas," she joked.

"Hey! You know I don't like being called that!"

Ash rolled her eyes.

"Anyways, let me introduce myself. My name is Billy Belima. I am your trainer."

"Um, hello, Mr. Belima," Kayla said.

"Please, call me Billy," Billy said.

"Okay, but what are we going to learn here?" Ash asked impatiently.

"Yes, I was just coming to that," Billy said, waving his hand around. "Here, we will be learning many things, but first, you must put your name down for the classes you would like to take. This is the list."

He handed them each a packet of paper.

The list was long, with the heading Training Classes on it. It included

Physics – 1

Chemistry – 1

Biology – 1

Arithmetic – 1

Algebra – 1

Geometry – 1

Data Technology – 1

Robotics – 1

Computer Technology – 1

Reading – 1

Writing – 1

Grammar – 1

Spy – 3

Mimicking – 1

Art – 1

Climbing – 1

Detective – 3

"Okay, so we can decide to do anything from here?" Nick asked.

"Yes, but there is a limit on how many people can do each class," Billy told them. "That is what the numbers mean."

"Okay," Ash said. "So, the ones with the number 3 mean that all of us have to do it, and the ones with number 1 mean only one person can do it?"

"Precisely," Billy said. "Now, how about you choose the ones you want to do. I recommend you do the things that you are already good at instead of something new, as we don't have much time to train. This way, you can get much better at whatever you know in the least amount of time. You each pick seven classes."

"Okay," Kayla said.

Billy put the list on a desk, and the triplets crowded around it and started whispering. Billy turned away.

After a few minutes, they reached a decision.

"Okay, we have decided," Nick said as they all turned around to face Billy.

"I will be doing physics, geometry, data technology, grammar, mimicking, detective, and spy," Kayla said.

"I will be doing chemistry, algebra, computer technology, reading, art, detective, and spy," Ash said.

"I'll take biology, arithmetic, writing, robotics, climbing, detective, and spy," Nick said.

"Great!" Billy exclaimed. "Now, let's start training! You guys will be training with your teachers for two weeks, and after that, you will be on your own because the trainers have to go and do something else."

"What teachers?" Ash asked. "Aren't you the trainer?"

"I'm one of them," Billy said. "Anyway, let me introduce you to Noah, Emma, Lucy, and Sam!"

CHAPTER FOUR: MEETING THE TRAINERS

"So, I have four assistants who know as much as I do, and they will also be teaching you," Billy informed them as four people walked into the room. "I will only be teaching you when all of you are together. This is Emma." He pointed to a woman with long brown hair and dark, piercing eyes. "She will teach chemistry, computer technology, algebra, reading, and mimicking. And this is Noah." He pointed to a tall man with red hair and cold, gray eyes. "He will teach physics, geometry, data technology, grammar, and climbing. This is Lucy." He pointed to a woman with short blonde hair and strict, light brown eyes. "She will teach biology, arithmetic, robotics, writing, and art. I'll be teaching spy and detective. And this is Sam. She does sports training." He pointed to a woman with long black hair tied into a ponytail and kind hazel eyes.

"Cool," Nick said, sounding bored. "Can we start now?"

"Yes, I was just coming to that," Billy said. "But first, I must give each of you a copy of the schedule."

"Okay, fine," Nick grumbled.

"Here you go," Billy said.

The chart said: Schedule for Nick, Ash, and Kayla

7:00 a.m.—Wake up

7:15 a.m.—Get ready

7:45 a.m.—Breakfast

8:15 a.m.—Morning exercise

8:45 a.m.—Short walk

9:00 a.m.—Physics, chemistry, biology

10:00 a.m.—Data technology, computer technology, robotics

11:00 a.m.—Geometry, algebra, arithmetic

12:00 p.m.—Grammar, reading, writing

1:00 p.m.—Lunch break

2:00 p.m.—Mimicking, art, climbing

3:00 p.m.—Sports training

4:00 p.m.—Spy

5:00 p.m.—Detective

6:00 p.m.—Homework

7:00 p.m.—Dinner

7:30 p.m.—Research on Dark King

8:30 p.m.—Get ready for bed

8:45 p.m.—Sleep

"Wait, so you make our whole day's schedule?" Ash asked.

"Yup, we do," Billy said. "This place is kind of like your school. You'll be here for most of the day."

"Okay," Ash said.

"Wait a second; we have to sleep by 8:45?" Kayla asked. "That means that we have to be in bed by 7:45. It usually takes us an hour to fall asleep."

"You need to get in bed by 8:45," Billy said. "We aren't adding the time it takes you to get to sleep."

"Okay," Kayla said.

"Do we get weekends off?" Nick asked.

"If you want," Billy said. "But I would recommend you practice and do research."

"Yeah, I guess that makes sense," Nick agreed.

"You can wake up anytime you want before 7," Billy added. "So, do you have any more questions?"

"Ok," Nick replied.

"Good," Billy said. "It is good that you guys came here at 8:30 because now it is 9. I have to go and get a large cappuccino now. Bye!"

"Um, bye!" Ash said. "Enjoy your cappuccino!"

"Thank you," Billy said, bowing. His electric blue pom-pom fell on the floor. "Oops. I dropped my donche-donche."

"Um, that's a pom-pom, not a donche-donche," Ash said. "What even is a donche-donche?"

"Whatever," Billy said as he left the room.

"Well, what do we do now?" Nick asked.

"The schedule says it is time for physics, chemistry, and biology, so I guess Ash will go to chemistry, I will go to physics, and Nick will go to biology?" Kayla wondered.

"Yeah, I guess," Ash said with a shrug. "There is just one problem. Where do we train? I mean, this place is so big!"

"We will help you with that," Noah said in a deep voice.

"Aaahhhhhh!" Nick, Ash, and Kayla screamed as they turned around.

Noah laughed.

"You are laughing?" Nick asked. "Seriously, this is not funny!"

"Yeah, I mean, you guys scared us!" Ash exclaimed. "Is it normal for people to come and tell you something behind your back in this place? That has already happened to us three times in the last thirty minutes!"

"Yeah," Kayla said. "Does this happen all the time around here?"

"Sorry," Emma said.

"It's okay, but try to be more careful next time," Nick said.

Lucy nodded. "But seriously, we should start."

"Okay," Emma said. "Noah, lead the way."

"Yup," Noah said. "Kayla, you will come with me, Nick with Lucy, and Ash with Emma."

"Okay," Kayla said.

"Training starts now!" Noah exclaimed. "Follow us to your first lesson."

And they followed.

CHAPTER FIVE:
PHYSICS

Noah walked to a door with 'Physics' on it, and Kayla followed. He put a gray card on a black scanner in the middle of the glass door, and it opened. Noah walked through the door. The cream-colored room had a white table, a chair, and many shelves with different devices, notebooks, whiteboards, etc.

When Kayla walked through the door, a bunch of rainbow-colored confetti burst out of the floor.

"Physics is one of my favorite subjects, so I added some cool effects for when a new person walks through the door," Noah said, looking at the confetti proudly. "It scans how much you know, so I know what to teach you."

He looked at Kayla, but all he saw was Kayla's mouth wide open. "Are you okay?"

"Of course not!" Kayla exclaimed. "I am standing in a place with super cool things! OMG! I have so many questions! What was that key card that you just used? How does this room look so cool? And how did you invent all these gadgets?" She started running around the room really fast, and she kept touching things and saying, "What is this, and this, and this, and this?" She ran so fast that everything started to fall down because of the wind. She was like a living tornado.

"Whoa, whoa, slow down, slow down, you just did all that so fast that I couldn't even see you," Noah said, raising his hands. "It is almost like you have powers or something."

Then Kayla saw a mysterious look on his face, and he seemed to be in another world. "What?" she asked, putting her hands on her hips.

"Nothing," Noah said, snapping out of his thoughts. "Okay, Kayla, I will answer question number one first. I just used a key card, and you will get one too once your training is over. Number 2, this room looks really cool because we all worked super hard on making it. All the rooms have a lot of technology. Number 3, we all made these; we didn't buy them. But anyway, let's start."

"Okay, so can we start on something hard because I already know Quantum Physics, which is pretty complex," Kayla said.

"Great," Noah said, "Oh, yes, I just want to let you know that Pegasus told me everything she knows about you, but I would like to know more details from you."

"Yeah, I know," Kayla said. "I'll just tell you the entire story 'cause I don't know what Pegasus told you and what she didn't. When we were five years old, our parents left us at home with a caretaker because they had to go on an important business trip but never returned. They left us with money, but the caretaker left after a few months. We tried to live with the money we had left, but we were running low on it. We had also started to get bored with school. Every year we have moved up by three grades. School was easy, and we were running low on money, so we pretended to be adults and got a job. That was when we were nine. We had to put sticks on our feet to make us look taller, and we wore disguises. We started going from job to job as we kept getting fired. Finally, we got this job. We weren't expecting it, but Pegasus knew all about us and still recruited us. Our parents never came back. We waited and waited, but they never came."

"I see," Noah said thoughtfully. "I am sorry."

"It's okay," Kayla shrugged.

"Anyways, let's get started, shall we?" Noah asked. "Well, today we will be building a mission suit."

Kayla's mouth dropped open.

"Now, we won't be making the entire suit in this class or all by ourselves, but we will be participating in it," Noah said with a smile. "Nick and Ash will be making it today as well. We will spend the entire morning making this suit in each class."

"OMG, OMG, OMG, OMG!" Kayla shouted with excitement and jumped up in the air. "Let's do this!"

"Cool," Noah said. "Now, we will use this fabric piece here in this class." He pointed to a dress. "We will be trying to find ways to make this fabric handle super fast speed, be able to phase through things, add a comms device to help us communicate with each other, be able to combine with the other suits, be able to fly to you when you say a code, and have a call for help button."

Comms were tiny devices that you put in your ears, and then you could communicate with other people wearing them.

"Wait, what!?" Kayla exclaimed. "This is amazing!"

"Yeah, of course, it is," Noah said.

"Who knew you could phase through things?" she asked. "This technology hasn't even been invented yet!"

"It has," Noah said. "It's 2045!"

"Oh yeah, well, I don't know how I can make this kind of stuff if I have never heard of it," Kayla said.

"Don't worry," Noah said reassuringly. "This is not as hard as it sounds. I saw that you had all the information from when you attended all your Physics classes when I scanned your brain. Just dig back into your memory and use that."

"Wait, why did you even scan my brain in the first place?" Kayla asked. "That's just creepy."

"Like I said, it is so that I know what you know, and I can teach you the right things," Noah said calmly.

"Okay, fine," Kayla agreed.

She started to work on the suit. She took out wires from bins, wrote down formulas on the whiteboard, and connected things together. Soon, she was done.

"Good job!" Noah exclaimed with a smile. "This is perfect."

"Thanks," Kayla said.

"Okay, now do the exact same thing two more times for Nick and Ash," Noah said.

"Okay," Kayla said. She worked on the two suits and soon was done.

"Great," Noah said. "Now, in our next class, we will continue our work. Now let's leave. Did you have fun?"

"You bet!" Kayla exclaimed.

"I am glad to hear that," Noah said with a smile. "Before lunch, we will meet with everyone to learn what they have been doing on their first day."

"Great!" Kayla said.

They walked to Kayla's next session.

CHAPTER SIX:
CHEMISTRY

Emma took Ash to the chemistry room. It was a gray room with shelves full of chemicals, whiteboards, a table and chair, and the periodic table of the elements plastered on the wall. As soon as Ash opened the door, a question sprang out of the wall in front of her.

"Whoa," Ash said, surprised. "Do I need to answer this before I enter?"

"Yup." Emma nodded. "I added it to see what level you are on. And don't worry, Pegasus told me about your history, so you don't have to lie to us."

"Yeah, I know," Ash said. "I'm glad she told you because I can't lie."

"Sometimes, not being able to lie is a good thing because telling the truth is always easier," Emma said. "Now, get on with your questions."

"Okay," Ash said.

She worked on the question and soon got the answer.

"Ten questions!?" Ash panicked.

"Yes," Emma said. "They will get harder and harder. But don't worry, you got the first one correct, so you should be fine."

"Okay," Ash said. Soon, she was done with all of the questions.

"Great job!" Emma exclaimed, looking at her tablet. "You got all of them right! Now tell me, was that hard, easy, or just right?"

"Well, it was kind of easy," Ash said with a shrug.

"Good," Emma said happily. "Now I know that you can learn hard things. So, today, we will be learning how to make something fascinating. We are going to make a mission suit!"

Ash's mouth dropped open. "No way!"

"Yes, way," Emma said with a laugh. "Now, I just wanted to let you know that we won't be the only ones making this. Kayla and Nick are also making it, and we will do this all morning. Right now, we won't be making the suit, but we are thinking of some chemicals that will help make the suit more efficient and have some sort of a shield around it so that chemicals can't go through it."

"Um, okay," Ash said nervously.

"You can do it," Emma encouraged her. "Those questions that you just answered were about this. You got all of them right, so just think back in your memory and make it."

"Sure," Ash said uncomfortably. She took some chemicals from the boxes and mixed them. Soon she was done.

"Wow!" Emma exclaimed. "You're done! Let me just quickly examine these, and then let's check." She took out a machine and scanned them. "Great job, Ash! How about you make two more of these for your siblings?"

"Sure," Ash agreed.

"Before that, do you mind going to Lucy and telling her, 'Dark Ness use Sad Ness'?" Emma asked.

"Sure," Ash said slowly. "But why? And what does that even mean?"

"It doesn't have anything to do with you!" Emma snapped.

"Um, are you okay?" Ash asked, surprised by Emma's harsh tone.

"I'm fine," Emma replied, taking a few deep breaths. "Can you just please give her the message?"

"All right," Ash agreed slowly. She left the room and was soon back.

"Thanks, Ash," Emma said. "Now, how about the rest of the chemicals?"

Ash worked on them, too, and finished quickly since she had already made the mixture once.

"Great," Emma said. "Now, how about we get to our next lesson since it's time to go."

"All right," Ash agreed.

"Oh, yes, I forgot to tell you, please come to the main room," Emma said. "We will be doing a presentation on what we learned this morning. It will be before lunch."

"Great!" Ash exclaimed. "I can't wait to see what Nick and Kayla have been working on!"

"Good," Emma said. "Now, let's go to our next session."

CHAPTER SEVEN:
BIOLOGY

Lucy and Nick went to the biology room. A Glic-Screen was attached to the door.

"It's a test to see how much you know," Lucy explained.

"Okay," Nick said slowly. "But can't you just open the door? I mean, doesn't this just take away class time? And why is there a Glic-Screen stuck to the door?"

"The Glic-Screen will transport you to a digital hospital, and you will find a patient there," Lucy explained. "You must treat the patient as fast as possible."

"Doesn't this take away class time?" Nick asked again.

"It is a test to see how much you know," Lucy repeated loudly.

"Oh, okay," Nick said. "What happens if I try to help the patient but make a mistake?"

"You get punched in the face," Lucy said happily.

Nick gulped. "Oh boy. Couldn't you just make it a little easier? First, you get punched in the face! I mean, like, who wants that? Second, what if you got hurt? You would have to go to the doctor. Third, this is just a waste of time."

Lucy shook her head and shouted, "Enough with the questions! Just start!"

"Okay, okay," Nick said. "You really need to control your anger."

Lucy's face started to turn an angry red color, and Nick winced.

"Okay, sorry," Nick said quickly. "I'm on it." The Glic-Screen turned on and transported him to a hospital. There was a patient with a broken leg.

Nick started to fix the broken leg and succeeded. The Glic-Screen gave him 20 points, and he returned. The door opened.

"There you go," Lucy said as she walked into the room. The room was gray and had a white table, chair, shelves with food, and diagrams of plants, the human body, different types of animals, and so on. "See, it wasn't that hard."

Nick rolled his eyes. "I never said it was."

"Yeah, well, it seemed as if you were trying to say that" Lucy argued.

"No, I wasn't," Nick said, glaring.

Lucy sighed. "Well, let me tell you what we are going to do. Today, we are going to make a mission suit. Kayla and Ash are working on it, and we are all making it this morning."

Nick's mouth dropped, saying, "Okay, so what do I need to do?"

"You need to make the suit so that the body will be able to handle all the weight and find a way to make some super tiny food that will have the complete nutritional contents of a proper meal," Lucy said.

"Okay," Nick said slowly. He took out books and started to read about how to make bite-sized meals. After that, he took some ingredients and created the food. Then he took out the suit and added some wires and comfort supplies to ensure the body could handle the weight. The fabric part of the suit had already been made. Soon he was done.

"Great job, Nick!" Lucy exclaimed. "You're done! Now, how about you start the next suit?"

"Sure," Nick said.

Just then, there was a knock on the door.

"Come in," Lucy called out.

Ash opened the door, panting. "Hi. Emma told me to give you this message. 'Dark Ness use Sad Ness.'"

Lucy looked a little scared and tried to hide it, but there was still a little fear in her eyes. "Thanks, Ash."

"No problem," Ash said as she went out the door.

"What did that message mean?" Nick asked.

"Nothing important, better start now," Lucy said.

"But it kinda seemed important," Nick argued, not letting go of the question.

"Just start!" Lucy exclaimed.

"Fine, fine," Nick grumbled.

Soon Nick was done with everything.

"Great job, Nick," Lucy said. "Now, we shall leave for our next session. Please ensure that you come to the main room for a presentation at the end of your sessions this morning. You, Kayla, and Ash will tell each other what you learned today."

"Okay," Nick said.

And they left for their next session.

CHAPTER EIGHT:

TEAM MEETING

It was just before lunch, and the triplets and their teachers had gathered in the main room. During the morning lessons, extra chairs had been brought in so all six could sit down.

"Is everyone here?" Noah asked.

Nick, Ash, and Kayla were seated at the back of the room, while Noah, Emma, and Lucy were in the front.

"Looks like it," Ash said.

"First, we will share our experiences with each other from our classes this morning, second, we will tell you something, and third we will take questions," Noah said. "By the way, only the teacher who was there for the first class will share the experience with the student. Nick and Lucy, can you go first?"

"Okay," Nick said with a shrug. "Today, I helped make the super-suit that we are all making. In biology, I made the suit so that the body could take the weight of the suit and made these tiny snacks that have the strength of a full meal. In robotics, I developed security features so that no other robot can control the suit, and there is this remote control that can control tiny drones with cameras. The drones are part of the suit but can detach themselves and go to places we want to observe. I made a calculator in arithmetic so that we don't have to do the math problems in our heads. And in writing, I developed a code language called Workojo, and I'll show you guys that later. It is in one of the pockets in the suit."

"Cool," Kayla said.

"Nick spent nearly half the class talking today, but he still managed to get all of his work done," Lucy reported.

"What?" Ash asked, surprised. "Nick talking? You're talking about our Nick, right? Or is this someone else?"

"Yeah … Nick usually is pretty quiet while we talk," Kayla agreed, nodding.

"Weird," Lucy said.

"Okay, as interesting as that is, how about Ash and Emma go next?" Nick asked, trying to change the subject.

"Okay," Ash said, not noticing the change. "In chemistry, I made chemicals that would make the suit more efficient and provide a protective shield. In computer technology, I made a tiny Glic-Screen for the top of the suit, where the mask is, that is voice-controlled. In algebra, I developed a complex problem that only we will know how to solve to open the Glic-Screen. And in reading, I made a translator for all known spoken and code languages in the universe."

"Great," Nick said.

"Ash did an excellent job by finishing her work quickly and accurately," Emma reported. "She also had time to give Lucy a message from me." She looked at Noah and Lucy suspiciously and winked.

"What message?" Kayla asked.

"Ash gave Lucy a very suspicious message, but Lucy refused to tell me what it was about!" Nick exclaimed.

"Can you guys please ignore that message?! For the last time, it wasn't for you!" Emma exclaimed once again.

"Okay, okay, fine!" Ash said, trying to calm Emma down. "Jeez, it was just a question!"

"How about we listen to the last report?" Noah asked. "Kayla, it's your turn."

"Okay," Kayla said. "In physics, I made the suit capable of phasing through things, of handling high speeds, and able to combine with the other suits so that instead of nine suits, the ones we made for each other would combine and turn into three suits. I also made communications devices that will allow us to communicate with each other and have the suits come to us when we say the code word. The suits will also have a button that will call for help. I made a code in data technology that will help with the Glic-Screen that Ash built in the suit mask. I made a coordinate grid in geometry to help us locate each other. In grammar, everything that you guys wrote down came to me on this device, so I could add all the capitalization and basically edit whatever you guys wrote."

"Nice," Ash said.

"Kayla was extremely excited and was very impressed by all the gadgets," Noah reported. "She did an awesome job during the activity."

"Great," Lucy said.

"Hey, that isn't fair!" Nick suddenly exclaimed. "Everyone got good reports except me! That shouldn't be allowed!"

"Hey, we just give out the facts," Lucy said. "You did well, but you talked a lot. It's true."

"Fine, whatever," Nick grumbled.

"After today, we won't be doing presentations following our training anymore," Emma announced. "This was just so you could see what your team members were doing in their classes."

"Now, we have something that we need to tell you, so, Noah, go ahead!" Lucy said.

"Why me?" Noah asked. "Well, we have to tell you that we will only be teaching you for two weeks, but whenever you need help, we will help you. We want you to get used to this place, not us. You will have to study all of your subjects. Billy will be the only one training you after two weeks, but that will be only for a small amount of time per day. You will be working on your mission for most of the day."

Nick, Ash, and Kayla's eyes brightened.

"Any questions?" Emma asked.

"I don't think so, but whenever we need help, we will make sure to call you guys," Kayla said.

"Yeah, definitely," Ash agreed.

"Uh-huh," Nick said, unsure.

"Thanks," Noah said.

"Anyway, I think it is lunchtime," Emma said.

"We should get going," Lucy said. "Follow us to the cafeteria."

They walked to the cafeteria.

"Wow," Nick muttered under his breath.

They all stared in awe as they looked around the cafeteria. The walls were a mix of blue, orange, and black. There were huge windows and several stations filled with almost every kind of cuisine, and the tables were made of marble.

"So, this is our cafeteria," Noah informed them. "It might take some time to get used to it."

"Um, does this place have vegetarian food?" Ash asked. "Cause we're vegetarian."

"Yeah, don't worry," Noah said. "It has vegetarian food."

"What about you, Kayla?" Nick asked. "You have not said a word for a minute, and trust me, that is really weird. Do you have any questions?"

Noah, Emma, Lucy, Nick, and Ash turned around. They saw Kayla at the Chinese station, putting almost every vegetarian item on the menu on her tray.

"Let's get some food before Kayla finishes all of it," Lucy said.

"I agree." Ash nodded.

The others nodded before heading to various food stations. They sat down and ate.

"Okay, guys," Noah said once they were all done. "It is time for us to work. You guys need to go to your sports class. We'll meet you again after it is over."

CHAPTER NINE:
SPORTS CLASS

"Welcome Nick, Ash, and Kayla to sports class," said a soft voice. "My name is Samantha Carpenter, but you can call me Sam. Here we will be learning all about how to fight."

The sports room was almost as big as a school gymnasium. It was orange and red, with weapons, balls, and many other things. There were two basketball hoops, one on each side of the room.

"So, today we will be learning the technique of ducking, leg-eye coordination, and using weapons," Sam said. "Based on your report cards, each of you is good at sports but at a different type of sport. Ash is good at racket sports like tennis and badminton, Kayla is good at running sports like soccer and basketball, and Nick is good at hand-fighting sports like karate and taekwondo. None of you have mastered the technique of weapon fighting yet. So today, we will learn how to fight with weapons. You will each get a Rayde, Gedlastic 2.0, and a shield. A Rayde is like a lightsaber, and a Gedlastic 2.0 is a laser gun. Both only stun, so don't be afraid."

"Okay," they all agreed. The triplets and Sam went to the blue-and-gray weapons rack, and each got their weapons.

"Now, let's start!" Sam exclaimed. "We will start by fighting with the Rayde. Instead of me teaching you how to fight with it separately, I want all of you to go against me at once because I want to see how you fight and how you think you should fight. After that, I will teach you what you are doing wrong as a group. So use the techniques you have seen in movies or read about."

"I guess," Ash said. "So, we just fight … you?"

"Yup!" Sam replied cheerfully. "Let's start!"

Nick, Kayla, and Ash raised their swords and charged at Sam, the tip of their Raydes facing her. Sam dodged Kayla's, blocked Nick's with her Rayde, and kicked Ash's leg. All three fell down but bounced back up. Nick charged at Sam again, but Sam moved out of the way, and Nick slammed into the wall. Ash slid down on her knees and went under Sam's legs, but Sam did a backflip and landed in front of Ash when she got up. Instead of fighting with Sam, Ash just fainted at Sam's backflip because it was so good. Kayla tried tripping Sam, but instead, she tripped herself and fell flat on her face. Nick got up, rubbed his forehead, and charged at Sam again. He kept charging at Sam repeatedly, but every time he tried, he bumped into a wall.

"Are you guys kidding me?" Nick exclaimed. "This is impossible!"

"Tell me about it!" Kayla answered.

Kayla decided that she wasn't that good at fighting, so instead, she decided to try to wake Ash up.

"Ash!" Kayla slapped her. "Ash!" She slapped her again.

"Huh?" Ash asked, waking up.

"There you are," Kayla said.

Meanwhile, Nick continued to charge at Sam.

"What is going on?" Ash asked, looking at Nick.

"Don't ask," Kayla replied, shaking her head. "Nick is going to be very sore for the next few days."

After a while, Nick got tired and sat down on the floor.

"Finally!" Ash exclaimed.

"Good job, guys," Sam said, wiping sweat off her forehead. "And thank you, Nick, for finally stopping to charge at me. I was getting exhausted. So, we need to work on our techniques. No offense, guys, but ... you don't know how to fight. Nick, you kept slamming into the wall, Ash, you fainted, and Kayla, you wouldn't even move. That calls for some serious practice."

"Yeah, we noticed," Nick said, rubbing his nose.

"How did you do that?" Ash asked, still in shock.

"Well, I have been practicing for a long time," Sam said. "Now, first, let me tell you some tips. During a fight, always stay focused. Keep fighting. Don't stop. Second, watch to learn your opponent's weakness. Third, practice your aim. Aim and strategy are the most important things in a fight. Just having power but no intelligence won't help you at all. And most importantly, never faint just because your opponent did something cool!"

"Got it," Ash said, knowing that the last rule was meant for her.

After some more practice and learning more about the weapons used in fighting, their skills improved. Soon, the class was over.

"Bye," the triplets chorused as they left the room.

"Goodbye," said Sam.

The three went to the training room and completed their remaining lessons with Billy. They ate their snack, did their homework—which was a sheet from every class they had that day—and ate their dinner. After that, they started their research on Dark King.

"As far as I know, there is no information I can find about Dark King," Nick said. He was at the main desk in their office, yawning and stretching his legs while spinning around on a chair to look at Kayla and Ash.

"I know," Kayla said, groaning and stretching, her chair on Nick's right side.

"It is so annoying," Ash said, echoing their groans from Nick's left side.

"Don't worry," Nick said. "We'll find something."

"I hope," Kayla said.

"By the way," Nick said, leaning closer, "I need to talk to you guys about something."

"What's up?" Ash asked.

"I think that Noah, Emma, Lucy, and Pegasus have some sorta dark secret," Nick said.

Ash rolled her eyes. "You think everyone has a dark secret. And none of them end up having one."

"I don't think everyone has a dark secret," Nick retorted.

"Uh, yeah, you do!" Kayla argued. "Remember when we worked at the grocery store? You thought that each customer was trying to steal the food! But it turned out they were just trying to get the watermelons that were right next to the exit!"

"And in the wood factory, you thought that our boss was trying to destroy natural habitat by putting chemicals on the wood, but it turned out that he was just trying to put food on it for animals to eat!" Ash said.

"And—"

"Okay, I get it, I get it," Nick grumbled. "But I'm sure about this."

"Okay," Ash said. "But we don't agree."

"Your choice," Nick said. "But I'm telling you, I'm right."

"Okay." Kayla shrugged.

Soon, it was time to go to bed.

"How about we wear the suits while we sleep?" Ash suggested. "I made them comfortable during art. And in an emergency, we don't even have to change!"

"Okay, sure," Nick said.

They changed into their suits and went to bed.

CHAPTER TEN:

MEETING THE GREAT VILLAIN

Two weeks later…

"Nick!" Kayla exclaimed, shaking him awake. "Wake up! It is our first day without training, and we can start our mission today!"

"It is only six o'clock in the morning," Nick grumbled.

"Actually, it is 7:30," Ash said, walking by.

Ash and Kayla had already gotten ready for breakfast, but Nick was still in bed. Nick immediately jumped out of bed. "7:30?" he exclaimed. "What? Is Billy mad? Does he know?"

"Don't worry," Ash said. "I only said that to get you out of bed, Nick. It is 6:00."

"Seriously, Ash?" Nick asked while Kayla and Ash burst into giggles. "Why did you do that?"

"Well, we wanted to eat our breakfast and do everything early, so we could start our mission," Ash explained.

"Billy said that we should go out looking for Dark King first and then train," Kayla said. "But remember, now we only have spy, sports, and detective training."

"Yes, yes, I know," Nick said. "And what mission?"

"I meant looking for Dark King!" Ash exclaimed, shaking her head.

"Oh yeah!" Nick remembered. "I knew that."

"Good," Kayla said. "Because then you will know that breakfast starts at 6:30 today."

"What!" Nick exclaimed again.

"Just kidding," Kayla said.

"Good," Nick said.

Nick got out of bed and walked out the door. Kayla and Ash followed but stayed a few feet away from the door. As soon as Nick put one foot outside their bedroom, an entire bucket of freezing cold water fell on top of him.

Kayla and Ash burst into laughter.

"C-c-ome o-n, y-y-ou g-uys!" Nick exclaimed, shivering, turning around, and heading to the bathroom. He wrapped himself with a towel.

"Sorry, we had to wake you up," Kayla apologized.

"Well, there had to be a better way," Nick retorted.

"There wasn't," Ash said, crossing her arms.

"Okay, whatever," Nick grumbled. "Let's go down for breakfast once we're ready."

Nick got ready, and the three went down for breakfast. After breakfast, they returned to their office and took out their research papers and weapons.

"Well, based on our research, Dark King has many servants and has a secret hideout where he has his weapons," Kayla said. "He also has many special powers. I think that he can freeze people, control people, he's immortal, and he can poison people by touching them, but he probably has more abilities that we don't know about. There is a special ancient rock that Dark King can use to kill everyone on Earth. Turns out, he has been looking for it for more than two thousand years!"

"Well then, we need to get it before him," Ash said. "Where do we find it?"

"Wait!" Nick said. "I heard of this rock when I read a book when I was five. It's called the Rock of Creation. It should be in the museum about two blocks from here."

"Wouldn't Dark King have searched there?" Kayla asked.

"Who would think that such an important thing would be hidden in a museum under thousands of people's eyes?" Nick asked.

"Good point," Kayla said. "But wouldn't he have read that book?"

Nick rolled his eyes. "It's a book for babies, Kayla. I read a part about the author, and it mentioned something about that."

"Good point again," Kayla said.

"So, what are we waiting for?" Ash asked. "Let's go get that rock!"

"I will attach a tiny camera to each of us so that whatever we do is recorded, and then we can turn it into a movie!" Kayla exclaimed. She attached a small camera to each of them.

"Okay …" Ash and Nick chorused slowly.

They grabbed their weapons from the sports room and went out of Mission Tech.

They started to walk outside. Soon, they heard a noise.

"What is that horrible noise?" Nick asked, cringing.

"I don't know, but I think we should follow it," Kayla said. "We have to postpone going to the museum."

"Okay," Nick said.

They followed the noise and soon came to a green park. There they saw a tall, bearded, dark-haired man wearing a gray suit and an eye patch. He was holding a sword and facing another man who was wearing armor.

"Sad Ness," said the man. "Find it!"

"I think that is Dark King," Ash said.

Dark King heard Ash. "Who dares to come and seek me out?" he asked in a dark, deep voice. "I am a king! I am the king of darkness, and my name is Dark King!" He spotted Nick, Ash, and Kayla. "Army! Kill them."

Suddenly, hundreds of transparent zombies with robot features flew from behind Dark King.

"Look out!" Kayla shouted.

Dark King and his army charged at them, shouting. The zombie ghost robots shot arrows at them, and Dark King threw swords, a new one appearing in his hand right each time he threw one.

"There are too many of them!" Ash screamed. "It is more than we can handle!"

"Well, we have to try!" Kayla said.

They took out their Gedlastic 2.0s and started shooting the zombie ghost robots. Unfortunately, nothing happened to them since they were not alive and were robots.

"Forget what I said about trying!" Kayla screamed. "Run!"

They started to run away from them. Kayla was in the lead, and Ash was close by, but Nick could not keep up with them. Arrows began to come near them. They all bounced off them since they wore their suits, but it still made them feel weak and helpless as they sucked away all the hope. The arrows were affecting their emotions, making them move slower and slower. Dark King started to follow them. He touched Nick, who collapsed on the ground.

"Nick!" Ash shouted.

Dark King and his army vanished and left them.

Kayla and Ash ran back to Nick.

"Nick, wake up!" Ash shouted.

They shook him. Nothing happened.

Ash pulled out her chemistry kit, took a sample of Nick's blood, and put it in the chemical, which turned green. Ash turned pale.

"What happened?" Kayla asked, coming to her.

"Nick has been poisoned," Ash explained, and Kayla paled.

"How is that possible?" Kayla asked. "We made the suits so that nothing can go through them."

"I know, so let's take him back, and then we can do some tests," Ash said.

Ash and Kayla carried him back to their office at Mission Tech. Surprisingly, Billy was waiting for them, drinking coffee.

"What happened?!" he asked, running over to them.

"Well, basically, we went after Dark King, and then he set some zombie ghost robots on us," Kayla explained. "We tried to shoot them, but nothing happened. Then, they started chasing us and shooting arrows at us. Nick ran too slow, and Dark King caught up with him. He touched him, and then Nick collapsed."

"That's not good," Billy said, concerned. "It's most likely poison."

"That's what we thought," Ash said.

"Well, you should probably run some tests on him and find an antidote," Billy said.

"Okay," Kayla said.

They went into their bedroom and placed Nick down on his bed.

Ash took a Toxicology test on Nick.

"Hmm, it seems as if the poison came from Dark King's skin," Ash said, staring at the test.

"I know… he must have used his power," Kayla said.

"Yup," Ash said. "Meanwhile, I'll try to see if I can find an antidote for him. I'm not that good with poison, but I'll try."

"Okay, good," Kayla said. "I'll try to fix the suit."

They started to work.

A few hours later …

"Great news!" Ash said. "I found an antidote. I wrote down the ingredients, but it's hard to get them. We will have to get some people to find the ingredients for us."

"I also have good news," Kayla exclaimed. "I figured out the components that I need to fix the suits. Now I just need to rebuild it, but I'll need your help."

"Great!" Ash exclaimed. "First, we should get the people to gather up the ingredients, then we can make the suit components! But the people will have to be from Mission Tech, or else we'll have to meet them outside of Mission Tech."

"Yup," Kayla said. "Let's get to work."

They started to call a few people. Soon after …

"Great news!" Ash said. "I found a person named Olivia who has all of the ingredients for the antidote in her office. She is bringing them here."

"Good," Kayla said. "Oh, look! She is here!" A woman walked through the door of their office, gave them the supplies, and left. Ash made the antidote as quickly as she could.

"All I need to do now is inject it into Nick's left arm," Ash said. "He will wake up as if nothing happened."

"Okay," Kayla agreed.

Ash injected the medicine into Nick, whose eyes slowly started to open. Then he got up.

"Where am I?" Nick mumbled sleepily. "What happened?"

"Well, you are in our office," Kayla said. She quickly explained what had happened.

"Wow," Nick said, getting up. "Well, we should probably go after him again."

"Not yet," Ash said. "You need to rest. Plus, it is lunchtime now. Maybe we can skip our lessons in the afternoon and look for him then, instead."

"But we have to take those classes," Nick said. "It is the rule."

"I know, but I think this is more important, and anyways you are the one who asked," Kayla said.

"I guess," Nick said with a shrug.

They ate their lunch, and afterward, they went back to the office.

"We need to get that stone before Dark King gets it," Kayla said. "I mean, like, he's looking for it already!"

"We'll have to break into the museum because how else are we going to get the rock?" Ash asked. "The museum people won't allow us to take it."

"Break into the museum?" Nick asked, shocked. "We can't break into a museum! We can get caught and go to jail, and… I can't go to jail! Nobody will trust me again, and I'll be humiliated, and-"

Ash rolled her eyes. "Relax, Nick. You're overreacting again! We'll be fine. We have been trained on how to steal for good purposes, so now we can use that training!"

"But we are terrible at stealing!" Nick protested. "We could get fired if we get caught!"

"That doesn't stop us!" Kayla argued indignantly. "We only get fired when we do something like blow things up!"

"Kayla is right," Ash said. "If we are going to save the world, we will have to steal it from the museum."

"Okay, fine, I get your point," Nick grumbled. "But we have to make a plan."

"Well, let's think of one," Kayla said.

"Okay," Nick said slowly. "But we've never stolen before."

"I thought you just said that you agreed," Ash said.

"Well, I guess I did say that" Nick said.

"Finally," Kayla said.

"So, now let's think of a plan," Ash said.

CHAPTER ELEVEN:

THE BIG HEIST

"So, I checked the museum blueprints, and the rock is in the East Wing," Nick said after about ten minutes. "And we'll have to enter at midnight because the museum closes at eleven. That gives us an hour to make sure no one is there. We can enter near the front and grab the rock. Now I know what you're thinking: if the camera sees any human beings, the alarm will go off, and the lasers will cut us in half. Don't worry! Kayla can hack into the cameras remotely after the museum closes. Got it?"

"Yup!" Kayla and Ash said.

Later that evening …

"Okay," Kayla said as she walked into the office in her mission suit. "I hacked into the cameras remotely, and they are turned off. But jeez, that was hard to hack through."

"Great!" Ash said. "Let's go!"

They left for the museum. Once they reached the parking lot, they saw some kids around their age walking nearby. They looked like them.

"Who are they?" Nick asked. "And why are they here? It's nighttime."

"They could be some other people trying to ruin our mission!" Kayla growled.

"I don't think so," Ash said thoughtfully. "Let's just continue."

They continued to walk. Once they came to the museum, Nick and Ash went in one direction, and Kayla went in the other.

"Where are you going?" Nick asked.

"I have a grand entrance I would like to make," Kayla said, straightening up and looking proud. "Don't follow me."

"Okay," Ash said slowly.

"But don't do anything dangerous," Nick said.

Kayla ignored Nick and walked away.

Once they reached the museum, Nick and Ash picked the lock and went to the East Wing. It was dark, so they turned on a flashlight. Suddenly, a hole opened up on the roof, and a rope came down. Kayla was on it.

"I am Kayla, the best thief in the world!" Kayla said, sliding down the rope and dabbing once she reached the floor. They were in a small brown hallway with tall ceilings and brown-tiled floors. The shelves were covered in clear glass, protecting the artifacts.

"Seriously, Kayla!" Ash exclaimed, with her hands on her hips. "That is your idea of a grand entrance?"

"I thought I told you that it shouldn't be dangerous!" Nick exclaimed. "And of all the ways you could have come, you come from there!"

"Well, this wasn't dangerous," Kayla said. "No one will know how I broke in, anyways."

"No one will ever know that there is a gigantic hole in the roof?" Ash asked sarcastically.

"Guys, stop arguing!" Nick exclaimed. "I have the rock, so let's go!"

"Already?" Kayla asked.

"Yeah," Nick said. "I took it when you and Ash were talking."

"Come on, let's get out of here," Kayla said.

Kayla tried to climb back up the rope, but she fell. Nick and Ash just watched.

"I think I'll just walk out the door with you," Kayla said meekly, and they headed for the door.

"There you are!" a deep, dark voice shouted. "I got confused with the other group."

"Who is that guy?" Ash asked. "We should probably just go."

"Where do you think you're going?" the same voice asked.

Nick, Ash, and Kayla turned around.

"Dark King!" they screamed. "Run!"

But before they had the chance to run, Dark King grabbed Kayla and held her close.

Kayla screamed. Nick and Ash turned around.

"Nick, give me the rock, and you will get Kayla, but if you don't … she dies," Dark King said, holding a ball of fire near Kayla.

"Nick, don't do it," Kayla said.

Nick looked at the rock and back at Dark King.

"Fine!" Nick said.

Dark King let Kayla go, and Nick gave him the rock.

Dark King vanished in a wisp of smoke.

It was silent for a while.

"Why, why, why did you have to do that?" Kayla asked. "You are risking seven billion lives!"

"I couldn't let you die," Nick said.

"But still," Kayla argued.

"Who cares about that?" Ash asked. "Dark King has got the rock of creation. Now he can do anything he wants!"

"Ash is right," Nick said. "Now we have to get the rock back."

"How about we research tonight and find out how the rock works?" Kayla suggested.

"Good idea," Ash said.

They returned to their office, turned on their computers, and started reading articles. After a couple of hours, they fell asleep.

The next morning …

Nick yawned. "Guys, I think we may have fallen asleep."

"Yeah," Ash agreed. "We must have been exhausted."

"How about we eat something and then continue our research?" Nick suggested.

"Okay," Ash agreed. They got up and got ready.

"Okay, now let's eat!" Nick exclaimed.

"Wait, where is Kayla?" Ash asked, worried.

"Let's look around," Nick said. "She could have woken up early and gone to eat breakfast. You know how much she likes getting up early, right?"

"Yeah, you're right," Ash said. "Nick, I will go get Billy. You go to the cafeteria and see if Kayla is there."

When Nick got to the cafeteria, he saw Kayla with piles of food in front of her.

"Ash, I found her," Nick said through the coms.

"Good," Ash said. "On my way."

Nick walked up to Kayla. "Hello, Kayla," he said to her.

Kayla jumped.

"Oh, uh, hi, Nick," Kayla said.

"Why are you eating so much food?" Nick asked sternly.

"Um, um, um," Kayla stammered. "Well, you can eat it too."

Nick raised an eyebrow. "Okay … sure."

He sat down next to Kayla as Ash walked into the cafeteria.

“We’re all eating it,” Kayla said before Ash could say a word.

“Okay, then it’s not a problem,” Ash said.

They all ate their food and walked out of the cafeteria. Just then, they heard a screeching noise.

“Guys, there is that noise again,” Ash said, panicked.

“I know,” Kayla said. “Why is it following us?”

“I don’t know,” Ash said. “But we must figure it out.”

“Well then, let’s go and find out who is making that noise,” Nick said. “We must follow the noise, and it will take us to him.”

“Okay, sure!” Kayla exclaimed.

“Let’s go!” Ash said.

“Where do you think you’re going?” a familiar voice from behind them asked.

CHAPTER TWELVE:

DARK KING'S HIDEOUT

"AHHH!" Nick, Ash, and Kayla screamed.

"It's just me," Billy said. "Where are you going?"

"Well, we're, um, going for, um, a walk," Kayla stammered.

"Okay," Billy said, not convinced. "But it is your lesson time. We have them today in the morning, as we have a special conference in the afternoon. You guys know that. Plus, you guys never miss your lessons to go for a simple walk. And you already went for a walk."

"Kayla, stop lying." Ash sighed. "We're going to stop Dark King."

Billy turned pale. "Why? You guys, like, just went yesterday. You should take a break and go another time."

"Are you Dark King?" Nick asked suspiciously.

"No, no," Billy said quickly. "Why would you think so?"

"Well, you don't want us to fight him," Nick said.

"Even though getting this bad guy is way more important than a lesson," Kayla added.

"We can do a lesson anytime, but we don't have the chance to catch Dark King anytime," Ash added.

"Well, I think you can get hurt," Billy said firmly. "Do you remember what happened to Nick just yesterday? I am just trying to keep you safe. Nick just got poisoned, and now you want to do this?"

"We'll be safe," Nick promised. "We'll be back by dinner time."

"What?" Billy asked. "I jus—"

"Bye!" Nick, Ash, and Kayla said as they walked out of Mission Tech.

After they had walked for a while, Kayla asked, "Where are we?"

"I think we are in a forest," Ash said.

"Yeah," Nick said. "Wait, who are they?"

Ash and Kayla turned to see who Nick was talking about. There stood three other kids who looked around their age.

"I say we talk to them," Kayla said. "We saw them yesterday at the museum, remember?"

"Yeah," Ash said. "We should ask them why they were trying to spoil our mission."

"Okay, sure," Nick said. "But let's be careful." Before approaching the other trio, the other kids walked up to the triplets.

"Hi!" a girl with tanned skin, short, wavy brown hair, and dark brown eyes exclaimed. "My name is Grace."

"Hey!" Kayla said.

"We wanted to ask you about what you were doing yesterday," said the other girl, who looked like Grace but was shorter. "By the way, I'm Nora."

"What *were* you guys doing there?" Ash asked.

"How about you tell us first," said a boy who looked similar to both girls but was taller. "I'm Chase."

"Fine," Nick said. "We were on a mission. Your turn."

"We were on a mission too!" Grace exclaimed.

"Really?" Kayla asked. "Maybe we can work together. My name is Kayla, by the way."

"Yeah, it would be great if we could do that," Nora said.

"Yeah, we are trying to stop Dark King," Ash said. "My name is Ash."

"Ash, don't give anything away," Nick hissed. "I am Nick, by the way."

"I suppose you're the mature one," Chase said.

"Yeah, how'd you know?" Nick asked.

"Because he is the mature one in our house," Grace said.

"Well, technically, it isn't a house," Nora said. "We live in the for—"

"Nora, stop!" Chase exclaimed. "We can't give anything away to these guys. Not even our you-know-what."

Ash raised an eyebrow. "What?"

"Nothing," Chase said quickly. "Okay, we've got to go. Can I just have your number?"

"Okay, sure," Kayla said. She gave him their number.

"Okay, thanks," Chase said.

"Well, bye!" Grace said. "Nice meeting you!"

"Bye!" Nick, Kayla, and Ash said.

"I wonder who they were," Nick said thoughtfully as they continued to walk. "I feel like I recognize them."

"Uh-huh," Ash said. "Guys! Look!"

Kayla and Nick looked in Ash's direction and gasped. They saw a giant spiral in the air that was pink, purple, and blue. It seemed to be sucking up air.

"OMG!" Kayla exclaimed. "A portal! We have to go through it! It might take us to Dark King's hideout!"

Nick shook his head. "It's too dangerous. We don't know where it could go. What if it goes into a lava pit or something?"

"Please, please, please!" Kayla and Ash begged.

"Fine," Nick grumbled.

They stepped through the portal and started twirling and twirling. Everything was blue for a while. Half a minute later, another portal opened up to a passageway. The triplets fell and hit the ground hard.

"Ow," Ash said. "That hurt."

They rose slowly.

"Where are we?" Kayla asked.

They were in a dark cave made out of rock with a gray tunnel leading out of it. The floor was made of brownstone, but it had some sand. It looked old like many people had been there. There were red glowing lanterns on the side that allowed them to see.

"I don't know," Nick said.

"Well, one thing I do know about this place is that it's dark," Ash said.

"Good thing I brought a flashlight," Nick said.

They started to walk.

"This place looks exactly like Mission Tech," Kayla said. "Maybe it is Dark King's hideout! That would be so cool!"

"Probably just a coincidence," Nick said. "This place is not Mission Tech because the smell is different."

"Yeah, but just in case, I'll take a sample of the sand here," Ash said.

"Okay, sure," Kayla said.

She took out gloves, a trowel, a clear liquid test tube, and a bag. She scooped up some sand and poured it into the test tube. The liquid turned green.

"This is the same thing that was on Nick's clothes when Dark King touched him!" Ash exclaimed. "I bet that this *is* Dark King's hideout."

"That's exactly what I said!" Kayla exclaimed. "From now on, you guys better listen to me! I was right about the entrance to Mission Tech being a secret passageway, and I was right about this!"

"Anyway, we didn't even have to walk here," Nick said, ignoring Kayla. "A portal just opened up for us."

"Yeah, I know," Ash said thoughtfully.

"Well, now that we're here, we don't have to worry, so how about we talk about something while we walk," Kayla said.

"Yeah," Nick agreed. "This place is similar to Mission Tech, so we'll just follow the same path."

"Good idea!" Ash said. "Now, what should we talk about?"

They were silent.

"How about we talk about who Dark King is?" Kayla suggested.

"Okay," Ash said. "Well, I think that Dark King is our old school principal."

"Yeah, for sure," Kayla said with a shudder. "He was so creepy."

"Actually," Nick said, "I think that it is Pegasus."

"What?" Kayla and Ash asked. "Really?"

"Well, that's what my instincts tell me," Nick said. "And they're almost always right."

"I don't know about that," Ash said. "Pegasus is a girl. Dark King is a boy."

"And we're at the end of the secret passageway, and there is a slide just like it usually is in Mission Tech, so let's go down the slide," Nick said, trying to change the topic.

"Okay," Kayla said. She paused. Then she asked, "You are changing the topic, right?"

Nick turned red. "Whatever."

They went down the slide. At the bottom was a long, dark staircase leading down.

"So, now we go down the stairs, right?" Ash asked.

"Seems like it," Nick said.

They went down the stairs. Then they saw a long white corridor with around ten doors on each side.

"Now, which door are we supposed to take?" Ash asked.

"We could find out, somehow," Nick said. "Ideas? Anyone?"

"Well, I could quickly run and check it out," Kayla suggested.

"Okay, but you aren't fast enough," Ash said.

"Seriously, you have no idea," Kayla said with a grin. She started to run, and it was as if she was just there, gone, and back again in the blink of an eye.

"There we go," Kayla said, panting. "We need to take the fifth door on the right."

"Um, thanks," Nick said, looking at Kayla strangely. "You know what? I actually think that we have powers."

"Well, if you want to know, Nick, we can do a DNA test and see if there is anything different," Ash said.

"Yes, yes, yes!" Kayla exclaimed.

"Okay, okay," Nick said. "Seriously, you don't have to get so crazy about it. The one that we're going to do is totally gonna hurt."

"I still want to do it," Kayla said.

"Anyways, we should go," Ash said. "We're running out of time!"

"Yeah," Nick said. "I am surprised that no one has seen us. Usually, there would be cameras everywhere."

"Well, I guess there are either no cameras, or nobody is looking at the security footage." Kayla shrugged. "Or they don't really care."

"I guess. Let's get moving," Nick said.

They went through the door, and they saw a machine that was being built. No one was there. The machine was gray and massive. It had a silver handle and a bunch of wires everywhere.

"Well, that was easy," Kayla said with a shrug.

"Now all we have to do is just take this machine back to Mission Tech, and then Ash and I can run some tests on it to figure out what Dark King is planning," Nick said.

"Yeah," Ash said. "But who is going to carry it? I mean, it is so big and made of metal so...."

"Well, no need for that," said a familiar voice behind them, "because you just missed your chance to get away."

CHAPTER THIRTEEN: BETRAYAL AND KIDNAP

They turn around.

"Noah?" Kayla asked, shocked.

Behind Noah, a second figure took off their hood.

"Emma?" Ash asked.

A third person also took off their hood.

"Lucy?" Nick asked.

Then a person who had been behind all of them stepped to the front.

"Pegasus?" the triplets exclaimed.

"What are you guys doing here?" Kayla asked.

"You don't know yet?" Noah asked in a sarcastic voice. "Why is nearly everything here the same as it is in Mission Tech? Why is all of the DNA the same? Why would we be here? You can't put the pieces together?"

"Well, technically, we just came here, and we don't know our exact location," Ash said. "We only know that this place is Dark King's hideout."

"Well, I thought that you guys are supposed to be smart," Pegasus said sarcastically. "I guess I made the wrong choice."

Something clicked in Nick's mind.

"So, it is you," he gasped. "You guys are part of Dark King's team. You designed this place. You knew everything about us. That is why you were so secretive."

"Took you long enough," Lucy said.

"Well, I kind of knew all along," Nick said.

"Well, we know more about you than you know about yourselves," Emma said.

"And now that you know all about us, you know we can't let you go, right?" Pegasus asked.

"Wait," Ash said, "you're going to keep us prisoner, here?"

"Yup," Noah said. "We're keeping you here till we're done with our work and our main purpose has been served. Then we'll let you go, but it will be too late by then. You won't be able to stop us. Also, we won't ever be going back to Mission Tech. We need to get our work done now without having any interruptions. And we'll be guarding you."

"You know we can't have you guys telling anyone our secret," Emma said. "You would do the exact same thing."

"But if you don't want to stay here like prisoners, you have an option," Pegasus said. "Join us. Join us and help us. We could really use bright minds like yours. We aren't the villains."

"You guys are the villains." Nick snorted. "Plus, why would we join you, of all people?"

Kayla and Ash felt betrayed. They had trusted Pegasus and their instructors. Even though Nick was proven right, he also felt surprised and disappointed because he had hoped that he was wrong (for once).

"Well, we'll just have to keep you guys in a jail cell, which is technically a room," Lucy said. "It's sad because I was hoping you guys would join us."

"Well, remain sad because we are never, ever going to join you guys," Ash said.

"Guards, tie 'em up," Noah said.

Suddenly, ten zombie ghost robots appeared from nowhere, tied them up, and threw them into a room, but the door was left open. The room was cramped, square with metal walls and a black-tile floor. There were no beds, and there was a small door at the back of the room that led to the bathroom.

"Um, I know that this is the wrong time, but who are you guys?" Kayla asked.

"Seriously, Kayla?" Nick asked. "You're thinking about people's names when you are tied up with no way to escape and nothing to do? Seriously?"

"Well, if you really want to know, we will show you," Pegasus said.

There was a burst of light, and they all transformed into another person. Pegasus turned into Dark King. Noah turned into a person who looked like Dark King but shorter. Lucy turned into a woman with long dark brown hair, brown skin, and a crooked nose. Emma turned into a woman with short-cropped blonde hair and a scar on her face.

"My name is Dark King," Pegasus said, with a dark, deep accent.

"My name is Dark Ruler," Noah said, with a growling voice and the same dark, broad accent as Dark King.

"My name is Dark Ness," Lucy said, with the same accent but not as deep.

"My name is Dark Chief," Emma said, with a mild touch of Dark King's accent.

"Why do all your names start with 'Dark'?" Ash asked. "Is it like a tradition or something?"

"Probably because they're all part of the same family," Nick said with a shrug.

"Um, Pegasus, you are a girl. Shouldn't you be, like, um, Dark Queen?" Kayla asked.

"I am a boy!" Dark King growled. "I just disguised myself as a girl."

"Oh, um, sorry," Kayla said nervously.

He rolled his eyes. "Whatever."

"Anyways, how about you tell us what your specific purpose is?" Ash asked.

"We all believe that darkness and evil can make the world a much better place," they said together. "Goodbye, Nick, Ash, and Kayla." And they vanished in a wisp of smoke.

The door closed, and the knots unraveled.

"Well, at least we don't have to stay tied to these chairs," Kayla said. She looked at Nick and Ash. They were looking down at the floor, dully and sadly. "What?"

"Nothing," Nick said. "It's just a lot to take in. Although I suspected their secret, I always hoped I was wrong."

"Yeah, same," Ash said.

"What do you mean?" Kayla asked with a laugh. "I know it is a little depressing, but you still got proved right, Nick!"

"But that doesn't mean I wanted to be right!" Nick exclaimed.

"I guess you are always right when you say someone is evil," Ash told Nick.

"Come on, guys!" Kayla exclaimed. "If I were you, I would be telling you guys a million times to believe me!"

"There is no way we will ever be her," Nick whispered to Ash.

Ash snorted. "Yeah, we won't. One day she will realize."

"Do you ever wonder what the dark secret is? Their dark secret is that their names all start with 'Dark'!" Kayla burst into laughter.

Ash and Nick just stared.

"So …" Nick said.

It got quiet.

"Awkward," Ash sang.

"Let's get out of here," Kayla said.

"But how?" Nick asked. "The bad guys or their army can catch us again! But we have to begin with trying to find a key because I see a keyhole on the door."

"Well, another option is that we could try to call Billy with the button you made," Ash suggested. She pressed the button on her suit, but nothing happened. "Ugh. This place probably has no satellite signal."

"Oh yeah, and none of us knew that!" Kayla said sarcastically. "Well, guys, since that did not work, we officially cannot communicate with Billy, so he can't come after us."

"I guess now we'll have to try something else," Nick said. "Or find a key, which is hopeless."

"Yeah," Ash said thoughtfully. "Any ideas? I don't have any."

"We'll find something soon," Kayla said. "Hey! How about we trigger the alarms, they'll come after us, and then we can escape!"

"McKayla Hall!" Nick shouted angrily. "That absolutely will not work! We could get severely hurt!"

"Let's just think of something else," Ash said.

"Fine!" Kayla grumbled. "I guess we can. And by the way, you don't have to yell!"

"Well, I had to because that was a horrible idea!" Nick said.

"Okay, I know she had a bad idea, but you don't have to yell about it!" Ash exclaimed angrily. "Only Mom and Dad called us by our full names."

"Yeah!" Kayla said. "The last time I checked, you weren't our parents!"

"But, while they are away," Nick said, "I was put in charge to take care of you guys."

"Yeah! But that doesn't mean you can yell at us!" Ash said.

"Ashley Hall!" Nick yelled angrily. "I was put in charge, so in the meantime, I can do whatever I want, and you guys must follow my orders!"

"Stop yelling at us!" Ash yelled angrily.

"Yeah, Nicholas Hall!" Kayla yelled and then giggled.

"You do not get to call me by my full name!" Nick barked. He scowled.

"Whatever!" Ash shouted

"Well, I've thought of a plan," Nick said. "We phase through the door and run out."

"Okay," Kayla said, "but that's not possible. One, there would be guards out there all the time. Two, if we leave, Dark King will come in and find us in a matter of seconds because there are sensors. And three, we can't move so fast. So, this plan is ruled out!"

"Okay, okay, no need to scream like that," Nick said. "We get it."

"Good, because you guys will never believe what I just found," Ash said.

"What?" Kayla and Nick asked as they came next to her.

"Well, I bumped my head against the wall," Ash said. "It was softer. So, when I turned around and saw that part of the wall, I saw this little bump. I pushed the bump, and it opened up into this pocket. I found something in there that looked like a key. It could be the key to getting out of here."

"Whoa, whoa, wait," Kayla said, interrupting. "You are just going over one of the best jokes ever! The key to getting out of here is a key! Get it?"

"Kayla, for the last time, this is not the time for jokes," Nick sighed. "We need to get out of here and fast."

"Yeah," Ash agreed. "Come on, let's try the key and run out."

"Okay, but if we are going to run, we have to make sure the coast is clear," Kayla said.

"Well, anyway, we need to have hope that this will work," Nick said.

"We just have to hope that it is going to work," Ash agreed. "And we can escape pretty easily."

"Actually, we won't," Kayla interrupted. "Remember I told you that this place has sensors?"

"Oh yeah," Nick said. "She said that if we leave, the sensors will get a notification, and then Dark King will be here in a matter of seconds."

Ash rolled her eyes. "Well, that was my only plan of getting out. Are you guys happy now?"

"Well, I have another idea," Nick said, ignoring her.

"Let's hope this one will work," Kayla muttered under her breath.

"What?" Nick asked.

"Nothing," Ash grumbled. "Just keep on going with your plan."

"Guys!" Nick exclaimed. "Hear me out. So, you two go out and find some supplies for arts and crafts. I'll stay here so that the alarm does not ring. Then, once you're back, we'll shut the door and make dummies of ourselves. Then, we can leave them here and get out."

"For the last time!" Kayla yelled. "The sensors will know the moment we step out of here!"

"If we go and come back quick enough, it probably wouldn't sense us," Ash said.

"Yup," Nick said. "It usually takes around ten seconds for a sensor to process whether a person has left. So, Kayla, if you can run fast enough, maybe you can get out, get the stuff, and come back before the sensor even knows that you have left."

"Then, actually, that's a pretty good idea," Kayla said. "But how do you know that?"

"I don't," Ash replied with a mischievous smile.

Nick slapped his forehead. "Well, I do. And I know that because I read about it one day. Lucy told me to make a sensor, so I had to read about them."

"Oh, okay," Ash said.

"The point is," Nick said, "my plan is a great idea. When you guys thought it wouldn't be."

"Yeah, because your plans are usually bad!" Kayla shot back.

Nick opened his mouth to say something.

"Let's just start before this turns into a fight," Ash said quickly.

"UhUh-huh Nick said, waving his finger back and forth at Kayla and Ash. "You guys are not getting away this time, so as I was saying, this is a victory for me." He started talking about how he was awesome, and everyone should listen to him.

While Nick was talking, Kayla and Ash got bored, so they opened the door. Kayla picked up Ash, and they ran right out.

"Hey!" Nick said when he realized.

While Kayla and Ash were outside, they discovered the room next door had some art supplies. There were no guards in the room or anywhere close to them, but the guards were heading their way. Luckily, Kayla and Ash were much faster. They ran into the room, took the art supplies, quickly returned to their room, opened the door, and rushed in, almost falling on top of Nick.

"Whoa, whoa, how are you guys so fast?" Nick asked. "And why did you run away while I was giving the epic speech about me?"

"Because when you talk about yourself, it gets boring!" Ash said.

"Correction: really, really, really boring," Kayla added.

"And it was weird," Ash said. "So we went out, got the supplies, and rushed back before the guards could catch us. Easy peasy. And we got back in less than ten seconds."

"Yup!" Kayla said. "I found this book, and it seemed pretty intre—"

"Why would you take the book? And why would you read it at a time like that?" Nick interrupted.

"Uh, is there a problem?" Kayla asked.

"The problem is that nothing ever really interests you unless it is cool like Mission Tech, and if it was cool, that means it is important! And if it is important, the guards will definitely notice that it is missing!"

"Ohhhh!" Kayla said, finally getting it. "Well, I like things that aren't really cool."

"And anyway, I took the book," Ash said. "It looked pretty interesting like Kayla said. I also saw a hacking device, so I brought it too."

"Are you trying to take the blame?" Nick asked.

"No," Ash said, offended. "It was about history, so Kayla wouldn't have really liked it."

"Like I said, are you trying?" Nick asked, repeating himself.

"Uh, I like history," Kayla said. "Who said I don't?"

"Everyone!" Ash and Nick yelled.

"Jeez, when did people start talking about me behind my back?" Kayla asked. "I don't know about you, but that is just plain rude. And you're wrong. I love history!" She crossed her arms, then she started talking with a heavy accent. "So, ha! Y'all talked behind mah back, but what y'all talked about got prooved wrang. Boom!" She punched a wrist forward.

Ash and Nick rolled their eyes.

"Can you at least tell me what it was about?" Nick asked. "So I know it was at least worth the trouble?"

"No," Ash said.

"Great!" Nick said sarcastically. "Just great."

"Now, all we have to do is make the models and leave!" Ash said, trying to change the topic. "We only need to use the hacking device to remove the lasers."

"Yup," Kayla said. "And once we get back, we'll really need to do a checkup."

"Yeah, don't worry," Ash said. "None of us have forgotten."

"Okay, I don't know about you, but I am really longing for a nice long walk outside, so how about we start building our models?" Nick suggested.

"Okay, okay, fine, fine, sure, sure, whatever," Ash grumbled.

"Whoa, whoa, wait," Kayla said. "That could be made into an awesome song!" She closed her eyes and sang in an extremely high-pitched voice, "Okay, okay, fine, fine, sure, sure, whatever. Okay, okay, fine, fine, sure, sure, whatever."

Nick and Ash covered their ears and cringed.

"Okay, that is pretty much the worst song I have ever heard," Ash announced after Kayla was done.

"And now, should we finally start?" Nick asked.

"Okay, okay, fine, fine, sure, sure, whatever," Kayla sang.

Nick rolled his eyes.

They started to work on their models. Those models didn't look exactly like them but definitely had a lot of similarities.

"Let's talk about something while we make our models," Nick said.

"Okay," Kayla said. "But what?"

Ash suddenly gasped.

"What?" Kayla and Nick asked.

"Nick, remember on our first day at Mission Tech, I came into the biology room and told Lucy, 'Dark Ness use Sad Ness'?" Ash asked.

"Yeah," Nick said, scrunching up his forehead.

"Well, she was probably just saying Dark Ness, which is Lucy's name, that she should use Sad Ness," Ash said. "I think that one of the people in their army's name is Sad Ness. And Sad Ness is probably the person Dark King was talking to earlier and said to find the rock. But obviously, as you know, they already found what they wanted."

"Yeah, you're right," Nick said.

"But why should she use that exact person in the army?" Kayla asked.

There was silence.

"I don't know," Ash said.

"Well, one thing that we know is that I was right," Nick said. "I knew that Pegasus was Dark King, and on our first day here, I knew that she was untrustworthy, so that is why you should always trust me."

"Kayla, you should not have told Nick that he should brag that he was right," Ash groaned. "This is like the hundredth time he's told us that!"

Kayla shrugged. "Well, at least he's happy."

They worked on the rest of their models in silence.

"Phew," Ash said after finishing her model. "We're done. Now, all we have to do is escape."

"Yup," Nick said. "And that'll be the hardest part."

CHAPTER FOURTEEN:

FAILED TRIES

"Good morning, guys," Kayla said the following day when the three awoke in their cell. "I don't know about you, but I'm starving."

They had slept on the floor since there were no beds.

"Well, good thing that I have these snacks," Nick said, taking the snacks out of his suit. "We can eat them." He took out the bite-sized meals he had made during his first day at Mission Tech, which were kept in the mission suit. Nick, Ash, and Kayla always wore their suits nowadays. They had made many of them washable so that they could wear one every day.

They all ate the snacks.

"Wow, that feels so much better," Ash said as they got up from the floor. "How about we try to escape today? If Kayla can go so fast, nobody should be able to see her or us."

"Yeah," Kayla agreed. "Let's try now."

"Okay," Nick agreed. "But we should be careful."

"Okay," the others agreed and quietly opened the door.

"Now, Kayla," Ash hissed.

Kayla picked up Ash, and Nick started to run. She ran through the hallway. Unfortunately, the doors in the hallway were all closed.

"Guys," Kayla said. "We have an issue."

"What?" Nick asked.

"Well, there is a door over there," Kayla said. "And it is locked."

"Well, just phase through it using the suit," Nick said like it was apparent.

"Okay," Kayla said. She tried to phase through, but it didn't work. Instead, she accidentally triggered the alarm.

"Uh oh, guys," Kayla said. "Now what?"

"Um, um, um," Ash stammered. "Maybe we could—"

"Hello, Nick, Ash, and Kayla," Dark King said, appearing suddenly. "Trying to escape? Don't worry, you won't get the chance. The doors are closed 24/7, and guards patrol the building all the time. The only thing you'll get yourself by trying to escape is torture and loss of hope. So today, our style of torture is fire. I will burn you!"

Dark King's hands lit on fire, and he threw some balls of fire at Nick, Ash, and Kayla.

Kayla felt tears pouring down her face. Ash's eyes filled with tears, but she blinked them away, and Nick's eyes started to water. But they needed to stay strong. They needed to escape. After a while, though, the pain was too strong to fight back, and Nick and Ash felt tears pouring down their faces. The fire didn't literally burn them; it just made them feel like they were burning and in a lot of pain. Soon, the pain became too much to bear, and they all fainted.

Nick woke up sometime later on the floor of their cell. He saw Kayla and Ash on the floor too. He couldn't bear to look at them.

"Kayla, Ash, wake up," he hissed. They both slowly woke and sat up, feeling weak and hopeless.

"What happened?" Kayla croaked.

Nick looked at her. "I don't know. We were wearing our suits. We shouldn't have been able to feel all that pain."

"Dark King's powers can go through our suits," Ash said. "But we must try again. We can't lose hope."

Kayla burst into tears. "But-but-but we just got tortured. I don't want to get tortured ever again."

"We must be strong, Kayla," Nick said gently. "We must be brave."

Kayla wiped her tears away. "We must be strong," she repeated quietly until she fell asleep.

"What should we do, Nick?" Ash asked. "This is not working out."

Nick stared out the window. "We must keep trying. We must not give up on getting our freedom."

Ash looked at Nick. "We need to improve our plan. The doors are shut, so we must improve our phasing. We must be ready for our next try."

Nick nodded. "We should let our bodies rest and heal before we try again."

"Okay," Ash said softly. "Let's sleep." And they all went off to sleep.

* *

"Good morning, everyone," Kayla said early the following day. Her eyes were red and looked like she hadn't slept very well, but she looked more like her old self.

"Good morning," Ash said with a yawn. "I think our bodies have healed already."

"Yup," Nick said. "They have. This is pretty fast, but it could have something to do with us possibly having superpowers."

Kayla nodded. "I feel normal already. We should try again today."

"But first, we must improve our technology," Nick said. "We must create a better phaser and fix the protection shield."

They all nodded.

"Well, let's do it," Kayla said. "I brought my tool basket. I shrunk it with a shrinking machine, so Dark King wouldn't find it. The zombie-ghost robots did search us when they threw us in the room."

"Okay, good," Nick said.

They started to work on the technology. Soon, the triplets were done.

"Okay, Kayla," Ash said. "Start!"

Kayla started to run. She ran faster and faster. Then, they reached the door. She tried to phase through, but again it didn't work. She once again triggered the alarm, bringing Dark King immediately after.

"Hello, once again, Nick, Ash, and Kayla. I see that yesterday's torture was not enough. But don't worry, you'll experience it again, but in a different form. I like to call it poison and freeze. It is my favorite. So first, I'll poison y'all like this." He held up his hands, and they all collapsed. "And then I'll freeze you." He did that again. He repeated the process again and again till they once more fainted.

After a while, Kayla woke up in their cell. "Ash! Nick! Wake up!"

They woke up slowly. "What happened?" Nick asked.

"It didn't work, I guess," Ash said. "The shield still must not be strong enough. But we should try again."

"What will he do next?" Kayla asked. "Throw us around the room with telekinesis? Give us a radioactive substance?"

Ash looked at Kayla. "Think positive. Everything will be alright. We've already healed. Now, we just need to improve our plan."

"I have an idea," Nick said. "We could hack into the security cameras using the hacking device, find a time when there are no guards by keeping a lookout, Kayla could work on her phasing, and try to make her move so fast that nobody can see her."

"Good idea," Kayla and Ash said. "But how long will this take?"

"I don't know," Nick admitted. "But no matter how long it takes, I know we'll get out. We just have to wait for the perfect moment."

"The perfect moment," Kayla repeated.

CHAPTER FIFTEEN: SUCCESS

The days passed, and soon they had been there for a week, then two. They continued to work on improving their escape plan and were waiting for the perfect moment, but they could never find a time when there were no guards around.

"Ugh, there is never a perfect moment to escape," Ash grumbled three weeks after their capture. "We've been here for ages!"

"Don't worry," Kayla said positively. "I'm sure that today will be the perfect day! You're the one who said to think positive!"

"Fine," Ash sighed. "Nick, it's your day to keep a lookout. You should probably take a look outside."

"Okay," Nick said as he quietly opened the door. "Nope, guards are still patrolling the area. I'll check again in about ten minutes."

While they waited, Ash read the book, *The Life of Darkness,* which was the book she had grabbed when she and Kayla went to get the art supplies. Kayla exercised and trained while Nick kept a lookout.

"Guys, guys!" Nick shouted later that afternoon. "The entire hallway is empty! This might be our only chance to get away!"

"Okay, okay," Kayla said. "Ash, let's hack in!"

They hacked into the security cameras.

"Now, Kayla," Ash said, "Run!"

"Great!" Kayla exclaimed. She planted her feet on the ground and, taking a few deep breaths, picked Nick and Ash up and ran as fast as she could.

"Whoa," Nick said while Kayla was running. "This seriously feels awesome. You've improved your running!"

"Thanks," Kayla said.

They ran through the hallway. Soon, the triplets approached the door.

"Okay, guys," Kayla said. "Let's phase!" Everyone turned on their phasers, and Kayla ran through the door.

"We did it!" Ash exclaimed once they had reached the other side.

"Shhh," Nick whispered. "Remember, they can hear us."

"Sorry," Ash muttered.

Kayla set Ash and Nick down. "You guys can run on your own now. The hard part is done."

"Okay," Ash and Nick agreed.

They kept running, not stopping once for a breath. They ran toward the exit. Suddenly, guards appeared on each side of the door! Then the hallway lit up with an eerie purple glow.

The guards wore red masks to hide their identities, and each wore a purple cloak. They also each had a sharp silver sword.

"Uh oh, what do we do?" Kayla asked.

"I'll go and fight the guards. You guys stay here," Nick said.

"Well, you will probably need some backup," Ash argued.

"Backup!" Kayla sang, dabbing.

"I don't need backup!" Nick said, putting his hands on his hips. He sang the word backup. "I will fight on my own!" He straightened his back and lifted his chin like a hero.

Ash rolled her eyes. "Yeah ... no. Can you just please take care of them?"

"Fine, fine," Nick grumbled.

"Me too?" Kayla asked, hopefully.

"Sorry, but no, I want to get out of here," Ash said.

"Anyway," Nick said, turning to face the guards. "Buckle your seat-belts, 'cause it's time to get fighty!" He curled his hands into fists.

"Really?" Ash asked. "That's your hero line?"

"Whatever," Nick said. He charged at a guard, punching him in the face, but another guard sneaked up behind Nick and tripped him. Nick bounced back up, spun around, and started punching and kicking guards, who fell down. Soon, only two guards were still standing.

Kayla nodded at Ash, and Ash returned it.

"Guys!" Nick said, looking at them, knowing they were about to do something mischievous.

"AAAAHHHHH!" Ash and Kayla charged the two standing guards from behind. They jumped on top of them and started tapping them on the head like they were playing the drums. The guards, still standing, were struggling.

"AAAHHH!" The girls kept screaming.

"*Okay, okay, fine, fine, sure, sure, whatever,*" Kayla sang as they tapped on the guard's heads to the beat.

"Guys!" Nick yelled at them.

"What?" Ash called down.

"Are you crazy?! Get down from there!" Nick yelled.

"Okay!" Kayla said.

Ash started to join in, and pretty soon, they were singing, *"Okay, okay, fine, fine, sure, sure, whatever!"* at the top of their lungs.

Nick slapped his forehead. "Oh my god," he said, shaking his head.

After much tapping, screaming, and singing, the guards were finally knocked out.

"Yay!" Kayla and Ash said, crashing to the floor as the guards they were on collapsed.

"You guys get excited about everything!" Nick grumbled, grabbing them both by the hands and leading them out the exit.

"Sorry, it's just that we like to have fun, and you don't," Kayla said with a shrug.

"Yeah," Ash agreed.

"Whatever," Nick muttered.

They walked out of the lair.

"Congratulations, guys, we're out," Nick said.

"Yes!" Ash exclaimed.

"Let's go back to Mission Tech," Kayla said.

"Yeah, we should tell Billy what happened," Ash said.

"Yeah," Nick agreed. "But after that, we must continue our mission."

CHAPTER SIXTEEN:
RESEARCH

The triplets returned to Mission Tech, sharing the news that Pegasus, Noah, Lucy, and Emma were really Dark King and his minions with everyone they knew. Finally, they headed to their office, hoping to find Billy waiting for them.

"Sit down, now!" Billy yelled as the triplets stepped through their door.

They quickly sat down.

"Where were you?" Billy yelled. "Do you have any idea how worried I was? I knew something like this would happen, but you guys did not listen to me! You also missed the most important meeting of the century! You are grounded for one month for your disobedience!"

"Well, technically, you can't ground us because you are not our parents, guardian, or the C.E.O. of Mission Tech," Ash said in irritation.

"No, I am!" Billy kept yelling. "Pegasus is evil, and she told the entire company that she was evil. I already knew that, and since you know, too, now I don't have to lie to you anymore! I am the boss now, and if you don't listen, you will be fired! This place is now called LMT, standing for Latte Mission Tech. Now I own the company, and I rule!"

"Latte Mission Tech?" Kayla asked with a giggle.

"Kayla, you're missing the point," Nick groaned. "Billy knew all about Pegasus and didn't tell us! But we should let him explain."

"Wait, you knew, and you didn't tell us?" Kayla asked.

"Well, that's just great!" Ash said sarcastically.

"Let's not get mad at Billy just yet. Like I said, he still hasn't told us why he did this." Nick crossed his arms.

"Fine, you have two minutes," Ash said to Billy.

There was silence.

"Well … why is it so quiet? Start explaining!" shouted Kayla.

"I didn't tell you because I wasn't sure they were evil," Billy explained. "Then I followed them around, and that is when I knew they were Dark King, Dark Ruler, Dark Ness, and Dark Chief. So, I confronted them, and I made them admit it to me. They did, and you were already gone when I got back. I tried to ask for answers, but they would not tell me. They said that if I told anyone their secret identities, they would kill you guys and me. But now I don't have to worry about that since they already told you. I am sorry that I didn't tell you sooner."

"We will accept your apology if you don't ground us," Ash said, her hands on her hips.

"Fine!" Billy cried, throwing his hands up in the air. He left.

"Well, let's get to work," Nick said. "We need to find a way to get some information since there aren't any websites or books we can go to or read."

"Actually, there is a book," Ash said nervously.

"What?" Kayla and Nick shouted.

"Yeah," Ash said. "Remember that book that I got from the art room in Dark King's hideout, *The Life of Darkness*? Well, that book is all actually about Dark King. There are a couple pages in the book that I wanted to tell you about."

"Okay," Kayla said.

"I'll read it out loud to you guys," Ash said, taking the book out of her pocket and flipping through the pages.

"Okay," Nick said. "How did you fit it in your pocket?"

Ash shrugged. "I shrunk it with Kayla's shrinking machine."

"Oh, okay," Nick said.

"Aha!" Ash exclaimed, stopping on a page. "Here it is!"

"Good," Kayla said impatiently. "Now start."

"Okay, chill," Ash said.

"A long time ago, when humans lived in caves, there was a big family in a cave. Twenty children and three adults sat outside on the golden sand, waiting for food. One adult was sitting outside and relaxing, one was reading a book, and one was cooking on a fire. The man cooking was the father of all the children, and the other adults were his siblings.

"When will the food be done?" a young boy asked, running up to the man making the food.

"Soon," said the man who was cooking with a kind smile. "I have a surprise for you today."

"Yay!" the boy shouted, running outside to tell the other children.

"Whoa, whoa, whoa, wait," Nick interrupted. "Are you sure that this is about our enemy? Because these people seem nice, unlike our enemies, who are mean."

Ash rolled her eyes. "Yes. Anyway, back to the story. Once the food was ready, the man gave it to the children and the adults. While they were eating outdoors, golden streaks of light started to wrap around them."

"Father, what is happening?" the boy asked.

"I don't know," the father said. Soon, the light streaks stopped.

"Father, I feel powerful," the boy said.

"I know," the father said. "I feel it too."

The father's face lit up as he realized something. "Whatever just happened has given us some sort of superpower! We should use it to make our world a better place!"

"Yes, yes," the children said. "We should!"

But the other adults disagreed. "We can't make the world a better place without making everyone agree with what we want them to do," said the woman, who had been sitting outside relaxing earlier. "And that could take away other people's freedom to choose what they want!"

"Yes, it is not right!" said the other man, who had been reading a book.

"Well, you may leave if you do not wish to follow us," the father said coldly. The man and the woman looked down with sorrow and left."

"Wait, wait, wait," Kayla said. "Who are these people?"

"I'll tell you later," Ash said. "So, the father later decided to make something only for himself. He mixed some ingredients together and came up with a potion. He drank it. From that potion, he got all the knowledge in the world. But the other man and woman took some of the potions by sneaking them while it was being made because they were thirsty. They drank it, too, and got all the knowledge in the world."

"Whoa," Nick said. "That's neat! I mean, if you know everything, you don't have to study for a single exam!"

"Yeah, and why would they want the knowledge when they said they don't want power?" Kayla asked.

"They didn't know it was the knowledge; they were just thirsty."

"Weird."

"Yeah, yeah," Ash said. "So, he built himself a spaceship and took off to a planet called Karkarus. Karkarus was a planet much like Earth, but bigger, less populated, and with better technology. The father thought it would be easier to build a colony there and make his plan to rule the world more accessible. The father and his children came up with a name for themselves. Most wanted to start with Dark because they thought Darkness was the right path.

"I will name myself Dark Star," the father said.

"I will name myself Dark King," said the boy, the eldest of all the children.

"I will name myself Dark Ness," a girl said.

"I will name myself Dark Ruler," another boy said.

"I will name myself Dark Chief," said another girl, and it went on till everyone was done. They lived in the city of Selijnowa. But during their stay in Karkarus, a bad thing happened.

"While Dark King was walking around town, a deadly snake bit him and poisoned his entire body! After learning what they could about the snake and examining Dark King, they realized that the snake's bite was fatal after 63 days. Only one antidote existed, and that took 97 days to make. Also, anyone who came within 241 feet of someone who had been bitten got sick too.

"But Dark King was saved, as the doctors in Karkarus had that antidote with them, and he got it before the 63rd day.

"Unfortunately, the potion that Dark King drank before coming to the planet mixed with the antidote, and the combination had a strange effect. He ended up with another power, the power to poison people by touching them. He even managed to share that power with his siblings. Earlier, Dark Star had gotten nearly all of the powers in the world. He has:

Light

Healing

Controlling machines

Nature

Super speed and strength

Teleportation

Marksmanship

Flying

Fire

Duplication

Immortality

Mind reading and control

Photographic memory

Time

Power absorption

Ice

Enhanced Senses

Growing and shrinking

Invisibility

Poison

Water

Rolling

Force fields

Transformation

Illusions

Telekinesis

Electricity

Knowledge

Laser

Power intensifier

Walking through walls

"His children had about 15 powers each. Though no one knows what they were."

"Whoa, he had like 30 powers! That's a lot!" Nick exclaimed.

"Maybe," Ash said. "So, once his son survived the snake bite, Dark Star got completely paranoid about one of his other children getting poisoned by the snake and not surviving. So he decided to leave the new planet and bring his children back to Earth with him. They all lived on Earth peacefully. During that time, he wanted to make his children more powerful. So, Dark Star came up with another potion that gave them the power of creation. He made yet another potion that made them immortal. Even though he didn't know it, he had just created the *Elixir of Life*, also known as the immortality potion. He also made a rock called the Rock of Creation, which held all of their power."

"Wait, they're immortal?" Kayla asked. "How can we beat them?"

"Yes, they're immortal," Ash said. She ignored the second question. "They needed to find a way to fit in with the rest of the humans. So, they decided to create many identities for themselves. Nicholas Flamel, for example, was actually Dark Star. As you know, Flamel was known as an alchemist. He is also credited with making The Elixir of Life and the Rock of Creation. He created many, many potions and wrote them down in a book. Many decades later, he burned the book because he didn't need the potions anymore and didn't want anyone else to find it. Not long after that, he disappeared. Some people believe that he might have been captured and taken to Karkarus by people who teleported from Karkarus to Earth and imprisoned in a dark place with no light, almost like a black hole inside a planet! It is used as the main prison there. It is called Zelosic, where Dark Star is being held because he did bad things, and some powerful people on Karkarus put him there. Some people believe the Karkarusians who put him there were the adults who disagreed with him at the story's beginning, but no one knows because they were disguised. Dark King is trying to rescue him. But to do so, he needs the rock which will allow him to go to prison. Now even though most people think that Nicholas Flamel is dead, he is alive, as Dark Star, because he is, as you know, immortal, and he drank his creation, The Elixir Of Life."

"Is that why he needs the rock?" Nick asked.

"Possibly," Ash said. "Anyways, during Dark King's search to find something to rescue his father, he decided to run for the president of the USA. While working, he could search people's minds and see what he was looking for since presidents gave many speeches and many people came to them. So, he manipulated people's minds and got elected president, using the name Erasmus Rotterdam, in 2028.

By 2029, the police started to steal, assault, and blackmail people. Dark King was ordering them to do it. Someone named Rufus Jackson confessed that he had hypnotized them to do it even though he didn't. Dark King controlled Rufus's mind the whole time and told him to confess. Some people thought that Rufus Jackson had done it, but some people were suspicious. They couldn't believe that Rufus Jackson had hypnotized them because he was good. Dark King was doing this so that while agents of the government were blackmailing people, he could go through their minds to find out if they knew anything about the book or the rock."

"Whoa," Kayla said. "So that was the Great Crisis we were learning about in school?"

"Yup," Ash said. "Anyway, in 2030, kidnappings increased. President Erasmus Rotterdam seemed to have committed all the kidnappings, detectives said, as all the people were in President Rotterdam's house, and his fingerprints were on all of the people's skin. They used a particular chemical to take it off people's skin. But he told them he had no idea about this, which was a lie. He had done everything. A few days later, someone named Philip Stoll confessed that he had committed the kidnappings. Dark King was also controlling him and forcing him to admit it. Stoll also revealed that he put the people he kidnapped in President Erasmus's office to frame him. But this was all a lie. Philip was taken to prison, but people stopped trusting the president. In 2031, President Erasmus Rotterdam went to New York City and disappeared. He was found ten days later, stuck in a library with locked doors. He was let out, but his memory was gone.

"From New York City, he went to London and bought something worth two thousand dollars. Less than three weeks later, President Erasmus was found dead on the cave floor. People also suspect that the other two adults named June and August, who disagreed with Dark Star since the beginning, were the ones who killed President Erasmus."

Kayla and Nick gasped.

"Why would he be dead?" Nick asked. "I mean, he's immortal!"

"Well, he must have been faking it," Ash said. "Anyway, detectives believe that Dark King stole the diary Dark Star wrote when he was Nicholas Flamel. It had been turned into a children's book, but only the person with Dark Star's blood could take it and read it for what it really was. The diary is in this book, but I haven't gotten to it yet. It had many algebra problems like 2a x 35 – 3t + 3a = ? but there was no answer to the problems. There was also a map in the diary. The map had the coordinates –12223 –9382048, but those coordinates do not exist on Earth. The only place it could be is Karkarus."

"In his diary, Nicholas Flames also talked about people's rights. Unlike many others, he spoke about men's rights, not women. He was also talking about how darkness protects you, unlike brightness. 'Anger and fear keep you alive' is one of his favorite quotes. He also had the word SINGH written in his diary and circled in red."

"Dark King and his siblings were driven to find a way to rescue their father. To do so, they had to open a portal to the prison. For this, they must harm all life. And therefore they are using the Rock of Creation to make all life on Earth vanish. They are also robbing people so that they can buy materials to make the potion, which will give them the two powers that they need but don't have. Now, as Pegasus Bleisti, Dark King can do all these things. Being the most respected person in the United States, he has access to all places."

"Wow!" Kayla said. "That is a lot of info to process!"

"Yeah," Ash said. "Now, let me show you a page we could use very much." She flipped through the pages. "Aha! That's it! This page is about a potion that can activate your powers."

Kayla and Nick's mouths dropped, and both started to speak.

"Let me finish what I am saying," Ash said quickly. "So, if we really have powers, this can activate them. But this potion will make us super sick if we don't. It is written in Flamel's alchemy book. The ingredients are water, glucose, sulfate, methane, urea, fluoride, sodium, radium, nobelium, curium, and europium. But like I said, it will only activate powers you already have in your blood. Dark Star created a potion to give powers, but nobody knows how to make it except him. And … that's all."

CHAPTER SEVENTEEN:

THE TELEPORTER, THE FUTURE, THE KINESIS

"Why didn't you tell us this before?" Kayla and Nick spoke at the same time.

"I wanted to finish reading the book," Ash said. "If I could, I would have read more pages to you at once. I only wanted to read the pages that were important to you."

"Fine," Kayla grumbled.

"Well, anyway, what is important now is that we know more about Dark King, and we've figured out that our main opponent is Dark Star," Nick said. "Kayla, how about you finish reading the book to get all the information. Ash, check to see if we have powers in our blood, and I will get the ingredients for that potion."

"Which potion?" Ash asked.

"The one that activates your powers," Nick said. "I'll just get them in case we have powers. We need powers to fight them and go to Karkarus, so…."

"OMG!" Kayla shouted. "We are getting powers! I want to have telekinesis, metamorphism, and super speed!"

"I don't think we can choose our powers," Nick said.

Kayla gave Nick an evil stare.

"Okay, no need to get angry," Ash said, patting Kayla on the back. "Yes, you actually can choose your powers because when your powers get activated, they are the powers that you dream of having. I read it in another part of the book."

"Whatever," Nick grumbled.

"Yes!" Kayla exclaimed. "We are getting powers!"

"Now, let's start," Nick said.

"Okay," Kayla and Ash agreed readily.

Ash squealed with joy only a few minutes later.

"What happened?" Kayla asked, coming over.

"We have powers in our blood!" Ash exclaimed, doing a happy dance. "I took the blood sample from Nick a while ago, put it in a Venumium, and then it turned purple, which means that we have powers! If Nick has powers, then we must too."

"Yippee!" Kayla exclaimed. "Now we can do research."

"Okay, great," Ash said.

"Hey guys, I found something!" Ash cried again half an hour later.

"You don't have to yell!" Kayla yelled back. "I am right here!"

"Sorry," Ash said. "Where is Nick?"

"Oh, he is out looking for the ingredients, remember?" Kayla said.

"He knows that the ingredients are in the building, right?" Ash asked.

"Eh, he'll get them somehow," Kayla shrugged.

"Anyway, I figured out what Singh means," Ash said.

"Really?" Kayla asked.

"Yeah, Singh is the last name of one of Dark Star's enemies. His first name is Earl," Ash said.

"Okay, so Earl Singh is the name of Dark Star's enemy?" Kayla asked.

"Yup. I also figured out some other things, but let's wait for Nick to return. In the meantime, I will go get some protective equipment for the potion. Kayla, can you do a live broadcast worldwide and tell everyone everything we've learned?" Ash asked.

"Okay," Kayla said slowly. "Why?"

"You'll understand later," Ash said.

"On it," Kayla said.

"Seriously, where is he?" Kayla asked as Ash walked into the room with the ingredients.

Kayla was on her desk chair, slouching and drinking lemonade while spinning around and around.

"You're done already?" Ash asked, confused.

"Yup, you sure took a long time," Kayla said.

"I was gone for only thirty minutes," Ash said, unconvinced.

"Well, to me, it felt like a million hours," Kayla said.

"Okay, well, where is Nick?" Ash asked.

"Here I am!" Nick said as he appeared through the doorway. His hair was ruffled, and he was covered in leaves and dirt.

"Hi Nick, what took you so long?" Ash asked, utterly oblivious to the dirt. "You know that all of the ingredients were in the building. But don't worry, I got them for you."

"Are you kidding me?" Dick started. "I went from store to store when Kayla was generous enough to finally call me and tell me the news!"

"Sorry," Kayla apologized. "By the time I had told you, it was too late."

"Anyway, I figured out something, so I think you might want to be sitting down for this," Ash said. "It'll take a while, and I don't want your legs to start hurting."

"Okay," Kayla and Nick agreed, sitting on the chairs at their desks.

"Dark Star made his own biography," Ash said. "He hasn't released it to the public yet, so I found the only copy in Pegasus's office. Dark King is going to release the biography after Dark Star takes over the world. It says that at the back of the book. Dark King was in it because he is Dark Star's son. Remember the cobra from my notes that poisoned Dark King? It appears they want to get all the cobras in the universe and suck the poison out of them. Once they do, they will be unstoppable and will destroy the universe. Their plan is to keep only one planet alive, which Dark Star will rule. Although they can just use the rock, only the people who have superpowers will still be alive. That's why they need the poison. Once he takes away all life, he will try to convince the superheroes to turn to his side, so he can rule much more easily."

"Okay," Nick said slowly, "so you're saying that all they need to do is free Dark Star? How will they ruin the universe with poison?"

"They will need to make a portal and make sure no one is alive to stop them, so they can use the rock," Ash said. "Everyone on Earth needs to be prepared. Kayla broadcasted a message on every single broadcast channel in the world. It also appeared on all devices, warning everyone about Dark Star and his servants. So, I don't think they will be able to leave. Troops are getting ready, and all of Mission Tech is on alert."

"Prepared for what?" Nick asked. "To die? And wow! How many things did you guys do while I was gone?"

"Well, I was reading the book, and I checked if we have powers in our blood, which we have. Kayla did the alerts, training, emails, and articles in like, ten minutes," Ash said. "Anyways, let's make the potion. Nick? A hand?"

"Wait, we have powers in our blood? But how? We can't unless our parents did; from what I can recall, they didn't have secret powers," Nick said. "Plus, if we had powers, our parents would have tried to activate them already."

"I didn't really think of that," Ash said. "But, we can think about that later. Now let's make the potion."

They left the room to make the superpower-giving potion.

CHAPTER EIGHTEEN:
DRINKING THE MILKSHAKE

"Well, here it is," Ash said as she and Nick walked into the room several hours later.

"Finally!" Kayla said, standing up from her chair.

Nick handed white cups to Ash and Kayla.

"Wait," Kayla said. "I thought we were drinking a potion. This looks just like a milkshake."

"I made the potion look and taste like a milkshake," Ash explained. "I didn't want us to be disgusted by it."

"Okay, guys," Nick said. "Three, two, one, go!"

They gulped the potion down.

"Ahhhh," Kayla said. "I feel strong and powerful. This is great. I can transform into anything, transform anything into anything else and mimic anything. I can move things with my mind and levitate. I can also run at super high speeds. I also have fast healing power and intelligence in specific things."

"Whoa, whoa," Ash said, stepping back. "How do you know all that?"

"Well, I just felt it," Kayla said, shrugging. "You guys just have to feel your powers."

"Okay ..." Nick and Ash said together. They both closed their eyes. After a while, Ash opened hers.

"Guys, I think you want to look at this," she said, sounding scared and nervous simultaneously. She had just shot ice out of her hands.

"Well, tell us your powers," Kayla said.

Ash closed her eyes. "I can go to the past and future and freeze time. I can control ice. I can take away other people's powers unless they have a shield around them. And I also can heal and have section intelligence, meaning knowledge in a specific area."

"Wow, cool!" Kayla exclaimed, jumping up and down a little higher than usual. "Now, Nick, your turn."

Nick tried to feel and think, and suddenly, he felt some warmth within him. "Now I know. I can turn into a rock and roll. I can teleport wherever I want. I can control fire and shoot fire. I can heal, too. And I also have section intelligence."

"Great!" Kayla exclaimed. "I just wrote all of this down. Here it is."

She showed them a paper. It said:

Our Powers

Kayla: Transformation, super speed, telekinesis, healing, section intelligence

Ash: Time, ice, power absorption, healing, section intelligence

Nick: Rolling, teleportation, fire, healing, section intelligence

"Nice job," Ash said. "Your handwriting has definitely improved."

"Hey," Kayla retorted. "I've always had good handwriting."

"Stop arguing! We need to think of a plan to stop Dark King from rescuing Dark Star," Nick said.

"Fine," Kayla and Ash responded, sulking.

"Ash, how about you go to the computer room and check some websites to find anything connected to Dark Star. Meanwhile, Kayla and I will try to work on creating a plan," Nick said.

"Let's get started!" Ash said, and she and Kayla left the room.

CHAPTER NINETEEN:
MEETING THEA

"Hi, guys!" Ash said in a cheerful voice as she returned to the room.

"Hi?" Kayla said, confused. "Why are you so happy?"

"I have a plan to stop Dark Star!" Ash exclaimed. "So, when I looked at some websites, I discovered something. A girl named Thea Reddit is Dark Star's adopted and betrayed child. Turns out she is intelligent, which is why Dark Star adopted her in the first place. She didn't know their secret until she became suspicious because they kept leaving the house and didn't for days. She looked around the house and found out some things that felt suspicious. When she saw that she had been used to advance their plan of destroying the world, she left. She took a lot of his money, bought her own house, and began living her own life. So, I say we ask her for more information about Dark Star and Dark King because we don't exactly know their plan. She lives in Bradenton, Florida."

"Great!" Kayla said. "Let's go!"

"We don't need to call a rideshare, do we?" Ash asked. "Since Nick can teleport?"

"I can't teleport to places that I don't have an image of," Nick explained. "When I teleport, I need to have a clear image in my mind of-"

"Yeah, blah, blah, blah, let's go!" Kayla exclaimed.

They called a rideshare service and headed for Bradenton.

"Well … this is it!" Ash said an hour later. They had pulled up at a tiny and broken house where all that was left was the garage.

"Should we knock?" Kayla asked.

"Probably," Nick agreed.

Kayla knocked once, twice, and three times. No answer.

"Well, she probably isn't here," Nick said. "What should we do now?"

When Nick said that, they heard a little crack and turned around.

"Hello," an old woman said. She looked fragile and wore an old run-down tracksuit, with a shawl wrapped around herself.

"Hi," Ash said. "My name is Ash, that's Kayla, and that's Nick. We came to ask you a few questions, and I swear it won't take long. May we come in?"

"Of course, come in," the old woman said.

They went inside and took a seat on the sofa. The triplets looked around. There was a bed, a chair, a kitchen, a couch, a TV, and more, all in one garage.

"You must be Thea," Kayla said.

"I sure am!" Thea said with a smile.

"We want to ask you a question about someone you might know … Dark Star?" Nick asked. "He's stuck on a planet called Karkarus, and we wanted to know if you know anything about that."

Thea's smile vanished, and there was silence.

"How dare you ask me about such a monster?" Thea asked furiously. "Get out!"

Before they could leave, Kayla quickly raced around the room. Unfortunately, both Ash and Nick saw her.

"What are you doing?" Ash hissed in Kayla's ear.

"I found some things out, now, don't talk to me, or I might forget them," Kayla replied.

Ash rolled her eyes.

"Can I use the bathroom?" Kayla asked Thea.

"Fine," Thea grumbled. "But do it quickly."

"We'll wait outside." Nick pulled Ash by the hand and through the door.

Kayla went to the restroom, took out a paper and a pen, and started writing as quickly as possible. Once she was done, she went outside to Nick and Ash.

"Wow, that was quick," Ash said. "I know you have powers, but can anyone use the restroom that fast?"

"I didn't use the bathroom," Kayla said. "While we were inside, I used my super-speed to run around the room, found notebooks, read them, found information, and wrote it down."

"Well, can we see what you wrote down?" Nick asked.

"Sure!" Kayla said. "But let's go back to our lab first."

Nick used his superpower to teleport them back to their lab.

"Okay, here it is," Kayla said.

Notes About Dark Star's Plan

Bad News

Dark King and his army used Thea so they could rescue Dark Star.

They have the Rock of Creation.

They will use it on Earth and create a portal to help their father escape the prison.

They need to kill everyone on Earth before they can make the portal, or else the portal won't work.

Once Dark Star is free, they will find all the cobras and become all-powerful.

Together, they will go planet by planet, killing everyone.

Thea also taught Dark Star to create his own galaxy.

His planet will be the only one remaining with life on it, and it will be called Aranchila.

We only have one month to stop them.

Good News

There is a way to reverse what the Rock of Creation does.

There is a way to trap Dark Star and everyone else that works for him.

To trap him, we must use the rock.

We just have to take the rock from Dark Star.

"Good plan, except we don't even know where Karkarus is," Ash said. "And this seems to be impossible. I mean, there is so much bad news and just a little good news? Come on!"

"Wait," Nick said. "We could just follow the coordinates that were there in Dark Star's diary. Y'know, the long ones that lead to Karkarus."

"Yeah," Ash said. "But how will we get there?"

"Well," Kayla said slowly, "we could teleport. I mean, what's the point of us having superpowers if we can't use them?"

Nick rolled his eyes. "I can't teleport anywhere if I don't know what the place I am teleporting us to looks like! There are, like, no pictures of Karkarus anywhere, so we can't teleport."

"Fine," Kayla grumbled. "How about we make a spaceship?"

Ash rolled her eyes and said, "Well, Karkarus is super far away. Experienced scientists have not found a way for a human to get to Neptune, which is relatively near Earth, but we can find a way to get to a place in another galaxy at the age of thirteen?"

"Well, we did figure out that we can do the impossible," Kayla stammered.

"Um, yeah," Nick agreed uncomfortably. "I can't believe I'm saying this, but Kayla's right."

Kayla stuck her tongue out at Nick.

"Sorry, but still no," Ash said. "Now, we need to tell Billy and start the mission."

They sent Billy a text alert.

Suddenly they heard a loud thud and looked at each other.

They rushed out of their office and looked at some cameras that showed huge world cities. They had just learned about the cameras that morning... People all over the world were disappearing in the blink of an eye.

"Dark King must be using the rock; that means his next step is opening the portal to Karkarus!" Nick said.

They looked outside, but everyone was gone.

"Wow, they're all gone," Ash said.

"Well, on the bright side, the Earth is saved!" Kayla said.

"Kayla!" Nick and Ash screamed.

"Well, there will be no more global warming, so we are all saved," Kayla said.

Nick rolled his eyes. "Kayla, there is no one to save Earth for!"

"Oh, then there is no bright side, just a dark side that Dark King and Dark Star are on," Kayla said sadly.

"Now, do you agree, Ash?" Nick asked, ignoring Kayla. "We need to get to Karkarus."

"Yeah, I'm in," Ash said. "But if something goes wrong, don't blame me."

"Seriously, Ash," Kayla said, shaking her head. "You are just so negative."

Ash rolled her eyes. "Well, let's get started. Kayla, during our exam to join the inventions company, you made the best rocket, so you can make that. Nick, you can get the supplies once Kayla knows what she needs and ensure that the human body can handle that much pressure. I'll make the fuel for the rocket ship."

"Okay," Kayla and Nick said, and they all got to work.

After a while, Kayla told Nick what she needed, and Ash told Nick what supplies she'd need to fuel the ship. Nick set off to gather what they needed.

"Okay, so while Nick is gone," Kayla said excitedly, "let's test out our powers! I know that you like a bit of fun, and Nick always stops us from doing anything dangerous. So let's try it out. Plus, we need something to cheer ourselves up."

"Okay," Ash said uncomfortably. "But, how do we do it?"

"Now that we know our powers, all we have to do is just, y'know, feel them like before," Kayla said with a shrug.

"Okay," Ash said slowly. "You go first."

"Okay," Kayla said.

"Move me with your mind," Ash said.

Kayla closed her eyes. She raised her hand, and Ash started to rise into the air.

"Whoa!" Ash breathed.

Kayla focused on Ash. "Can I put you down now?"

Ash raised her eyebrows.

"What? I'm only starting; I need training!" Kayla informed her.

Ash rolled her eyes. "Now use your super speed to go to Egypt and back and bring me a rock from a pyramid to prove it."

Kayla raced to Egypt, grabbed a rock from the sand, and raced back. She looked hot and sweaty. "Bad idea. It was so hot there."

She handed Ash a brown rock.

"Yup, this is from Egypt," Ash said. "Good job."

"Thanks," Kayla said.

Kayla continued to test her abilities, then Ash started to try hers as well.

"Okay, I want you to go back to 2019 and get a piece of technology from there," Kayla said.

"Sure," Ash said. She created a time portal and went through it. She got out and saw the world back then. "Whoa," she mumbled. "Things were so boring then." She went to a store and found a phone. "Boring. Where is the holographic screen? There is just this weird glass thing and a button. Weird."

She created a time portal and came back.

"You got it?" Kayla asked.

"Yup," Ash said. "And things were so boring back then. They didn't have any holographic screens, the buildings look weird, and … well, you get the point."

"Sad," Kayla said. "Let me keep what you got."

"It's called a phone," Ash explained as she handed it to her sister.

"Huh," Kayla said. "Apple, Microsoft, and Google were popular back then too. How old are they?"

"I don't know," Ash shrugged. "Anyway, what should I do next?"

"Hmmm, how about … Make an ice sword?!" Kayla said with excitement.

"Okay."

Ash thought about a sword. She lifted up her hand, and an ice sword sprung out of it. She threw the blade at the wall, and it went right in the center of one of the many targets they hung all over the room.

"Cool!" Kayla breathed.

"I know," Ash said in awe.

They kept on going, testing their powers over and over again.

* * * * * * * * * * *

Nick walked into a plant shop and ran to the bathroom, which was white but very, very dirty. He shuddered and closed his eyes, concentrating on making a portal. Slowly, a pink, purple, and blue portal formed, and Nick went through to an industrial plant. There were chemicals in tubes everywhere, and gas was coming out of the floor.

Suddenly, five of the same people from Dark King's hideout attacked him from behind. He turned into a human ball and rolled around on the floor at the speed of sound. The guards chased after him. Nick stood up, and fire came into his hands. He threw it around, purposely missing the guards. The guards got scared and ran away. Nick quickly got the chemicals they needed and teleported back to the lab.

"Hey guys, I'm back," Nick said.

"Great," Ash said. "Now, let's start."

They went out to the massive backyard of Mission Tech and got to work. By the time it was dark, they were covered in black oil.

"Okay, guys," Kayla said. "I think we should continue working now, so we can finish as soon as possible."

"Yeah," Ash said. "We need to finish it as soon as possible."

"We need to save the world fast," Nick said. "As soon as possible."

CHAPTER TWENTY:

NAMES

"Good morning, folks," Kayla said, getting out of bed a week later. "Now that the ship is done, we should start to pack and aim to leave tonight."

"Okay," Nick and Ash agreed, getting out of bed. "But what should we pack?"

They got ready and had to make their own breakfasts as nobody else was there. Then they started packing.

"Okay, so maybe we should wear our suits, so they don't take up space in our luggage," Nick said. "We'll have to pack an astronaut suit, two pairs of regular clothes, super suits, the tiny snacks I made, communications watches, a computer, batteries, a bunch of water, a first-aid kit, a toolbox, a sewing kit, and medicines for each of us. We don't need to pack anything for sleep because we already added it, but we will need our research papers, plus a notebook and two pencils for each of us."

"Okay," Kayla said, writing everything down on her clipboard. "That's a lot of stuff, but fine. I'll go pack this stuff. You guys should ensure that all super suits are still working."

"Okay," Ash agreed.

Kayla went to get the things from the list and soon was back. "Here you go," she said, throwing the super suits to Nick and Ash.

"Thank you," Ash said. Nick and Ash started to examine the suits while Kayla packed everything else. Soon they were done.

"Okay, I've packed everything," Kayla said, holding three heavy bags.

"The suits seem to be in perfect condition," Nick said.

"Good," Ash said. "Now, let's make sure that the ship is in a perfect condition like yesterday and make sure it still works."

"Yup," Nick agreed. "I'll carry the bags inside. You guys check out the controls."

They went inside the rocket. Nick arranged the bags while Kayla and Ash went inside the control room.

"Okay, all clear," Ash shouted from inside the control room after thoroughly examining the controls.

"Great," Nick shouted back. "I just finished arranging."

"Awesome," Kayla said, coming into the storage room. "Well, how about we say our tearful goodbyes and then leave for Karkarus!"

Ash rolled her eyes. "How about we do a not-so-tearful goodbye? Plus, who will we say goodbye to?"

"Oh yeah," Kayla remembered.

Just then, the girls heard a sob and turned around.

"Nick?" Ash asked. "Are you crying?"

"No, just got something in my eye," Nick said, tears pouring out of his eyes.

"Aww, is little Nicky crying?" Kayla asked in a baby voice.

"No," Nick retorted.

Kayla and Ash gave each other a look that meant *What's up with him?* and shrugged.

"Whatever," Kayla said. She raised her hand into the air and started to levitate. "We need superhero names!"

"Um, why?" Ash asked.

"Cause I want one," Kayla replied like it was obvious.

"How about we think of that later, like after we defeat Dark Star?" Nick asked.

"Fine, fine," Kayla grumbled. "Well, let's go!"

They went inside the ship and got into their seats. The rocket had a massive control room with many buttons, three black seats, white walls, a black floor, five bathrooms, three bedrooms, and a lab.

"Ready?" Nick asked.

"Ready," Kayla and Ash said.

"Well, let's take off," Nick said.

The three counted down from ten " … Five! … Four! … Three! … Two! … One!" they shouted together.

The rocket ship rose into the air, higher and higher.

"Ahhhhh!" the three screamed. Soon, the rocket ship was out of Earth's atmosphere.

"Whew," Kayla said. "That was not how I expected it to be."

"Totally," Ash said. "That was way faster."

"Well, it was fun," Nick said.

"Yeah," Kayla and Ash agreed. "It was."

"Well, now what should we do?" Ash asked.

"Like I said, superhero names!" Kayla said, lifting her hand into the air.

"Fine, let's think about our powers; maybe that will help us think," Ash said.

"Okay, we'll do Kayla first," Nick said.

"How about The Suthesis?" Ash asked after they had all thought for a while. "It's a mixture of telepathy and telekinesis."

"Nah, sounds pathetic," Kayla said.

"You *are* pathetic," Nick said with a smug smile.

Kayla stuck her tongue out at Nick.

"Okay, how about The Kinesis?" Ash asked. "It means movement or motion, and it comes from telekinesis."

"I love it!" Kayla exclaimed. "From now on, call me Kinesis when we are on a mission. We need to get our superhero names on our mission suits! My superhero symbol is three horizontal lines because that shows movement, and Kinesis means movement."

"Okay," Ash said. "I'll add it once we're done with all of our names."

"Let's do Ash next," Nick said.

"Okay," Kayla said.

They all thought for a while.

"How about Ice Queen?" Kayla suggested.

"Horrible," Ash said, shuddering.

"How about The Future?" Nick suggested.

"That is perfect," Ash said. "My symbol is going to be a fast-forward symbol. Meaning two triangles."

"Cool," Kayla said. "Now, Nick."

They all thought.

"How about Firport?" Kayla suggested.

"Um, no thanks," Nick said.

"Teleheat?" Ash suggested.

"Nope, on a rope," Nick said.

"Nope, on a rope?" Ash asked. "Seriously?"

"Hey, I'm just trying to say something cool," Nick said with a shrug.

"Anyways… how about The Teleporter?" Kayla suggested.

"Works for me," Nick said. "My symbol will be a portal."

"Can we decide our superhero team name, too?" Kayla asked.

"Sure!" Ash exclaimed.

They all thought again.

"How about The Spy Superheroes?" Nick suggested.

"Weird," Kayla said.

"How about The Super Superheroes?" Nick suggested again.

"Horrible," Ash said. "Now Kayla and I will think. Your suggestions are horrible."

"Fine," Nick grumbled.

"How about The Strong Superheroes?" Ash suggested.

"Weird," Kayla said.

"The Powerful Superheroes?" Ash suggested again.

"Nah," Nick said.

"How about The Tech Superheroes?" Kayla finally suggested.

"Okay, but we barely do anything with tech," Nick said. "It would just be weird."

"Well, don't ask me." Kayla waved her hands in front of her. "But it's the best thing we've got."

"Well, we use a lot of technology, I guess, and Ash and I used a bit of science and technology for the potion that we drank to get powers," Nick mused.

"Technology?" Ash asked.

"Yeah, you can use technology, even if you don't put it in the potion," Nick said like it was obvious.

"Huh?" Kayla asked.

"Just go with it!" Nick exclaimed. "We can keep the name."

"Yeah, sure," Ash said.

"Yay!" Kayla exclaimed. "What should our team symbol be?"

"How about a brain with different sections highlighted in the color our suits will be?" Nick suggested.

"Weird," Kayla whined.

"Fine," Nick said.

"How about three circles with our suit colors on it?" Ash suggested.

"I don't know," Nick said slowly. "We aren't exactly circles. Plus, it would be too big."

"Um," Kayla said, thinking.

"How about a big circle with all our logos inside it, so everyone knows what team we're on?" Nick suggested.

"Works for me," Kayla said.

"It's good," Ash said.

"Can we change the color of the suits to our favorite colors?" Nick asked.

"Okay," Ash said.

"Mine should be turquoise," Kayla said.

"Mine should be orange," Nick said.

"Mine will be purple," Ash said. She painted the suits they were wearing, including their individual symbols and the team symbol. "Now I'll go and add it to the other suits," Ash announced. She left and was back in a couple minutes.

"We're going to need a mask," Nick said. "The mask should be our favorite color and have our symbol on top."

"Okay," Ash said. She left again, but soon she was back. "Okay, guys. I've made the basic structure. Now Kayla and I are going to add the controls."

"Cool," Nick said.

"Nick, can you press the button for us to make our first light jump?" Kayla asked.

"Okay," Nick said.

"Wait, we added light speed on this?" Ash asked.

"Yeah, didn't you know that?" Kayla said.

"I was busy making the fuel, so no, I didn't notice," Ash said.

"Weird," Nick said. "You don't know what your own sister has been working on. Sad."

Ash stuck her tongue out at Nick. "Well, I'm leaving. Kayla, come on."

Kayla and Ash headed for the ship's lab and returned in an hour.

"Okay, we finished the suit," Ash said. "Here they are!"

Kayla's suit was turquoise and had full sleeves and full pants. There were light streaks of magenta on top. She had a magenta cape behind her. Her logo was in the middle, and on top of it was their team symbol. Below her logo was her superhero name, and their team name was below the team symbol. She had purple boots. Her mask was turquoise, and it also had her logo on it.

Ash's suit was purple and had full sleeves and full pants. There were ice blue lines on top. She had an ice blue cape behind her. Her logo was in the middle, and above it was their team symbol. Below her logo was her superhero name, and their team's name was below the team symbol. She had ice blue boots. Her mask was turquoise.

Nick's suit was orange and had full sleeves and full pants. There were light lines of red on top. He had a red cape behind him. His logo was in the middle, and their team symbol was on top. Below his logo was his superhero name, and their team symbol's name was below the team symbol. He had red boots. His mask was also red and had his logo on it.

"Cool!" Nick exclaimed.

"Guys, there is a planet that is flying," Kayla said, pointing out the view screen.

"What?" Ash said.

They looked where she was pointing, but suddenly the planet was gone.

"Eh, it's probably nothing," Ash said.

"Yeah, probably," Nick said.

"Guys, we're about to crash!" a familiar voice exclaimed.

They turned around.

"Billy?" Nick asked. "What are you doing here? You are supposed to be dead!"

"Well, I have my ways," Billy said. "Now, will someone please go get me the biggest latte possible? And who is driving the ship? We're about to hit an asteroid!"

"Oops, sorry about that," Kayla said. She ran to the controls to turn on the autopilot, then returned to the group.

"I'll also go get the latte," Kayla said. "Don't want to tire out the oldies."

Nick and Ash rolled their eyes at Kayla.

Soon, Kayla was back. "Here is your latte. It's the biggest one I could find."

"This…This! I cannot take this; it is so small! You need to get me at least a hundred of these!" Billy said.

"*Are you kidding me?*" Kayla asked. "I cannot give you one hundred more! You could die from the amount of caffeine there is! Wait a second, you could die! Then we won't have to keep up with you! I'll get them for you right away." She left and was back in the blink of an eye. "Here are your lattes!"

"Thank you!" Billy said. He drank them and then fainted.

"Now that's much better!" Kayla said.

She looked at Nick and Ash. Their mouths were wide open, but they couldn't speak. Ash couldn't make a sound, but Nick recovered quickly.

"Are you kidding me? Did you kill him?" yelled Nick. "This is the only human being other than us who is alive, and you killed him!"

"Relax," Kayla said. "I didn't kill him; I warned him! But I didn't want him to die, so I just mixed some of Ash's chemicals together, and voila, he fainted. So, you're welcome," Kayla said and bowed.

Now Nick fainted.

"Wait a second, what chemicals did you add?" Ash asked.

"Um, I don't know," Kayla said. "I make lattes so often that my brain was working subconsciously, and you don't remember many things you do from your subconscious, so yeah."

Ash turned pale. "Let me check." She took out her chemistry kit and took out a sample of Billy's blood. "You put a radioactive substance in Billy's blood?" she cried, and she, too, fainted.

CHAPTER TWENTY-ONE:

FIXING BILLY

"Ash, Ash, wake up," Kayla said, shaking Ash awake.

"What happened," Ash mumbled.

"You fainted," Kayla said. "Because Billy almost died."

Ash gasped. "He must be dead by now! We need to take him to a hospital!"

"Number one," Kayla said. "We are in space, so there is no hospital. Number two, you just woke up from fainting, so you probably don't know what you're saying. Number three, I fixed Billy up after you and Nick fainted. He's fine now."

Ash sighed with relief. "Good. Can I see him?"

"Sure," Kayla said. She took her to the emergency room.

Ash screamed when she saw Billy sitting on the bed with a bunch of wires dangling from everywhere.

"Hello," Billy said. "How may I help you?"

"What did you do to him?" Ash screamed at Kayla.

"Um, I fixed him," Kayla said. "I gave him the antidote that I found on the Internet. It was the only one. Unfortunately, this one had the side effect of losing your memory. There is an antidote for that, and I tried to make it, but I couldn't. That is why I woke you up, so you could make it."

Ash shook her head. "If you just hadn't made the coffee, none of this would have happened."

"That's the thing, right?" Kayla said. "Billy is in the subconscious part of his mind right now. When I was in mine, I couldn't remember anything either. But then I remembered coffee and went to get it for Billy. So, all we need is the right trigger."

Ash looked at Kayla strangely. "When did you learn so much about biology? You were horrible at it in school."

"Well, I talked to Nick for a while," Kayla said. "He told me everything, and then he went back to sleep."

"Nick woke up?" Ash asked.

"Yup," Kayla said. "I needed help, so I put a very smelly shoe under his nose, and he woke up. Unfortunately, he was still tired, so he went to bed, taking a nap."

"How much did he tell you?" Ash asked.

"Not much, just how to hold Billy until you woke up," Kayla said.

"Well, to take the radioactive substance out of Billy's blood, I will have to scan it with a special machine I made, and then, when we know where it is, we will rip open his skin and suck it out," Ash said.

"But what about the antidote I already gave him?" Kayla asked.

Ash shook her head. "The radioactive substance you gave him made him faint and lose his memory. All you did was make him wake up, but the radioactive substance is still there."

"What about pulling the right trigger?" Kayla asked.

Ash slapped her forehead. "Kayla, the radioactive substance is still there. We can only pull the trigger after the radioactive substance is gone."

"Oh, okay," Kayla said. "Then why did the Internet not say any of this?" Private satellites followed them around in space, allowing them to get an Internet connection.

"Kayla, you can't believe everything you read on the Internet," Ash said. "Plus, not all the information about what you're looking for is there."

"Oh," Kayla said. "Okay."

"Now I'm going to scan him to check where the radioactive substance is," Ash said.

"Wait, how do you know so much about biology," Kayla asked.

Ash slapped her forehead. "I did a one-year course in advanced biology; remember when we skipped all the grades and went to college when we were six? Nick did it for three years, though."

"Oh, yeah, right," Kayla said.

"Okay, now let's start," Ash said. She removed a machine from the cabinet and put it above Billy's feet. She started there and kept moving the device up his body. Then, when she reached his stomach, she stopped.

"I think I found it," Ash said. "The radioactive substance was digested, and it's in his stomach. It's spreading pretty fast." She took out two knives and handed one to Kayla. "Okay, now I have to suck it out before it infects anything else. Kayla, how good are you with a knife?"

CHAPTER TWENTY-TWO:
PULLING THE TRIGGER

"You want me to help you?" Kayla asked.

"Yeah, why not? I'll need the help," Ash said.

"Yeah, but we have to cut him open!" Kayla whined. "Plus, I'm horrible with a knife."

"We?" Ash asked. "Oh no, we are not going to do that. Is that what you thought? Because I meant we just have to use the knife to open the machine. If anyone is going to cut him open, it's Nick."

"Hello, how can I help you," Billy interrupted.

Ash looked at Kayla. "Go and wake Nick up. I'll open the machine."

"On it," Kayla said.

Kayla went to wake Nick up while Ash broke open the machine.

"Nick, Nick, wake up," Kayla said, shaking Nick awake.

Nick's eyes opened.

"We need your help," she said. "You need to do an operation."

Nick jumped out of bed and ran to the infirmary section of the ship. He saw Ash opening up the machine. "Are you done?" he shouted.

"Yes," Ash said.

Nick ran up to Billy and started the operation.

After three hours, he was done.

"Phew," Nick sighed with relief. "I'm done. Now, all we have to do is find the trigger to release Billy's memories."

"Good," Kayla said happily. "How about you guys go and do that while I fly the spaceship."

"Okay," Nick and Ash said.

Kayla went to fly the spaceship while Nick and Ash tried to find the trigger for Billy's memories.

"Hello, how may I help you?" Billy asked politely.

"Hmm, so what should we say?" Ash asked.

"How about coffee?" Nick suggested. "He seems to really like coffee."

"Okay," Ash agreed. "So, we just keep on repeating it?"

"Yup," Nick said. "Now, let's start."

"Coffee, coffee, coffee, coffee, coffee!" Nick and Ash chanted. "Coffee, coffee, coffee, coffee, coffee!"

Nothing happened.

"Um, this is not working," Ash said. "Should we try latte? Or cappuccino?"

"Latte," Nick said.

"Latte, latte, latte, latte, latte!" they chanted again.

Billy answered, "How can I help you?"

"Ugh, this is not working!" Ash grumbled.

"Don't give up hope," Nick told her. "Let's try a cappuccino."

They chanted that, too, but nothing happened. Nick and Ash kept repeatedly trying until…

“Okay, now let’s try Billy Belima,” Ash suggested desperately.

“Billy Belima, Billy Belima, Billy Belima!” they chanted.

“Yes, yes, yes,” Billy said, getting up. “Why are you chanting my name so many times? And why am I wrapped in so many wires?”

“Billy!” Nick and Ash exclaimed, running over to Billy and wrapping him in a hug. “You’re back!”

“Kayla, come here!” Nick shouted.

Kayla ran into the room. “I’m here!” she shouted. She turned around and saw Billy. “Billy! I am so sorry that I lost you! I made you leave us!”

“I was never gone,” Billy said. “I was just in the subconscious part of my mind. And it’s good that Kayla did that because I figured out many things.”

“What did you find out?” Kayla cried.

“I figured out,” Billy said darkly. “That I am Sad Ness.”

CHAPTER TWENTY-THREE:
SAD NESS

"Sad Ness?" Mindy asked. "As in, 'Dark Ness use Sad Ness?"

Billy nodded.

The triplets backed away from him.

"Now, now," Billy said. "I was not Sad Ness by choice. I was controlled."

"Controlled?" they chorused again.

Billy nodded again. "Dark King made a special machine to control me. He was able to send my mind from the conscious part to the subconscious part. Then, he controlled me. He sent me to the subconscious part because he didn't want me to remember anything."

The triplets gasped.

"He can do that?" Kayla asked.

Billy nodded. "Yup."

"Whoa," Kayla gasped. "Cool!"

"Anyway," Billy said. "I know their plan."

"Well, good news," Ash said. "We already know their plan. We spoke to Thea, and Kayla sped around the room using her superspeed and found things she used to write down Dark Star's plan."

"Huh?!" Billy exclaimed. "Speed? Huh? What are you talking about?"

"Uh, guys!" Nick stammered, pulling them into a huddle in the corner of the room. "We never told Billy about our powers, did we?"

"Nope!" Kayla said.

"So ..." Ash said, pulling out of the huddle. "Yeah, we already know the plan."

"Oh, okay," Billy said disappointedly.

"Actually, we need to know something," Nick said. "On our first day of training, Emma told Ash to go and tell Lucy, 'Dark Ness use Sad Ness.' We never knew what she meant, so can you tell us?"

"Hmm, let me think," Billy said. He searched through his mind. "Dang it! I will need to go back to the subconscious part of my mind to do that."

"But, but, but, we just lost you," Ash stammered. "We can't lose you again."

"Actually," Kayla said. "We could try to make the same machine that Dark King made."

"Oh, yeah, but how?" Nick asked.

"You should know," Ash said. "Come on, let's go read some books about it and make the machine."

They left the room and went to the lab. They read some books and made the machine. It had a band that went around the head and a computer that showed what was happening in the person's mind.

"Back!" they exclaimed. Ash plugged it in, and Kayla put the band around Billy's head.

"Stop, stop," Billy said. "You're touching my donche-donche."

"Sorry," Kayla said. She put it around Billy's head so it didn't touch the pom-pom hair band. She turned the machine on and searched for "Sad Ness." The machine spun through memory after memory until it found a scene. It paused there, and the memory played on the screen. Ash and Nick were busy fixing the wires, so they couldn't see what was happening.

Kayla saw Billy, dressed in armor, following Dark King's instructions.

"Sad Ness," Dark King said. "Open up the portal to Karkarus."

Sad Ness took the stone out of his pocket and threw it into the air. Then a portal opened up. Dark King and his siblings went through it. After it closed, the stone fell to the ground and broke into a million pieces.

"No, no, no," Kayla groaned. "No, no, no." And she fainted.

CHAPTER TWENTY-FOUR:

LANDING ON KARKARUS

"Kayla, Kayla, wake up," Ash said, shaking Kayla awake.

"What happened?" Kayla mumbled.

"You were just groaning, and then you fainted," Nick explained.

"What did you see?" Billy asked.

Kayla repeated the memory, and Billy turned pale.

"Wait, you're saying that the stone is broken, and Dark King has gone to Karkarus?"

Kayla nodded. "If we don't have the stone, how will we make the trap?"

"But, I still don't get why I had to be used," Billy groaned.

"We'll figure that out later," Ash promised. "First, we need to get the rock."

"Yeah, we do," Nick agreed.

"But the portal was opened on Earth, right?" Billy asked.

"Actually," Kayla said, "it was opened on Karkarus. The portal to get to Karkarus had to be opened by killing nearly everyone, but the one I saw was the one that opened on Karkarus so that they could rescue Dark Star. The stone only works twice, and then it needs to be fixed by a person with a particular special power. You can't get to the prison where Dark Star is kept unless you're on Karkarus."

"Okay," Ash said slowly. "So where, exactly, did they open it?"

"I don't know," Kayla said. "Karkarus is five times bigger than Earth, and we don't even know our way around."

"Oh," Ash said. "Right."

"Well, before we get too negative," Nick said, "how about we go and book a hotel so we can live somewhere?"

Kayla snorted. "Yeah, we can, after we reach Karkarus. And if they even have hotels."

* *

A few days later, an alarm started blaring throughout the ship.

"What is that?!" Billy asked.

All four were all in the infirmary area.

"It means we are in for a crash landing!" Ash exclaimed.

"Quick!" Nick shouted. "Ash, Kayla, follow me. Billy, stay here."

Nick, Ash, and Kayla ran to the control room and quickly sat in their chairs. They looked at the engine room through the cameras that they had added.

"It looks like one of the engines is breaking down!" Kayla exclaimed.

"We just entered the atmosphere. That must be why," Ash explained.

"But why would the engine break?" Nick asked. "We made it indestructible!"

"Well, we don't know the pressure of the atmosphere because we have never been here before!" Ash exclaimed. "So, it still could have broken!"

"Guys!" Kayla exclaimed. "Can you continue this conversation later? We are crash landing here! The engine is breaking even more!! See?"

They all got up from their chairs, and Kayla pointed around the room. The alarm blared even louder, casting a red light all around the ship.

Suddenly the spaceship started to shake.

"Aaahhhh!" Ash yelled. "Grab onto something!"

They all grabbed onto one of the beams on the side of the control room.

The ship started turning, and Nick, Ash, and Kayla were thrown all around the ship.

"We'll have to use our powers on the ship to stop it from turning!" Ash yelled through all the chaos.

"Okay!" Nick and Kayla yelled back.

They wrapped their legs around the pole to look like they were sliding down it.

"Can you teleport me to the engine room?" Ash asked Nick.

"Sure," Nick said, making a blue-purple portal to the engine room.

Ash pulled her legs from around the pole and pushed off it, heading toward the portal.

"Ouch," she grumbled, landing headfirst in the engine room. Suddenly, she flew up and grabbed onto the edge of the plastic around the engine. The engine was a gray metal cylinder with yellow and red wires sticking out. One part was broken, and Ash lifted one arm from the plastic and pointed it toward the engine, spraying ice everywhere to freeze the parts.

"Ash?" Billy asked, flying into the room.

"What are you doing here!?" Ash exclaimed.

"I fell off my bed," he said, embarrassed.

"Oh, well, now is not the time for this conversation!" Ash said, still freezing the engine.

"Focus, Ash!" Billy yelled.

"I can't focus if you're telling me to!" yelled Ash.

"You can do it, Ash!" Billy yelled.

"Just be quiet!" she yelled back.

There was complete silence.

"I did it!" Ash yelled.

"Yay!" Billy exclaimed.

"Let's go back to where Nick is," Ash said.

A portal appeared, and they both went through it.

* *

"Can you also teleport me outside of the spaceship?" Kayla asked Nick, hanging onto a poll to ensure she didn't fall, back in the control room.

"Okay," Nick said. "What am I? A teleporter? Everyone uses me for transportation!" he muttered.

"Well, your superhero name is The Teleporter, so-"

"Just be quiet!" Nick yelled.

He made another blue-purple portal that led to the outside of the spaceship while Kayla transformed herself into a person wearing an astronaut suit. She used her telekinesis and flew into the portal. Soon, she was outside of the spaceship, which was shaped like an airplane and had "Latte Mission Tech" written on it.

Kayla moved carefully, the spaceship's gravity supporting her as she went to the top of the spacecraft. She floated a little above it, then closed her eyes and concentrated, holding her hands out with pressure. She moved her hands around and kept them stable. Suddenly, the ship stopped turning, and some of the ship had ice around them. Slowly, the ship started to stabilize. Kayla continued to work to keep it that way. She guided the ship toward the ground of the nearby planet. When a portal appeared, she pushed off the ship and went through it.

* *

After Ash and Kayla returned, Nick pushed off the pole with all his strength and turned into a ball, pushing against the force, pulling him away, and moving toward the controls. He unwrapped himself and grabbed onto the edge of the control table, pulling himself up and sitting in his seat. He used his firepower to fry the alarm and the emergency situation button (ESB). The ESB was self-activated, and whenever the alarm rang, it went into emergency mode, dropping the ship toward the nearest ground. The alarm stopped, and everything became quiet.

The engine was fixed, and the ship headed toward the ground, meaning that Ash and Kayla had correctly fixed what they had to do.

"Yes!" Kayla exclaimed. "We did it! Now we just have to find a hotel to stay in! I do not want to sleep on this ship! I want to explore!"

"Wait," Ash said.

"What?" Kayla asked.

"It isn't safe for all of us to go," Ash said. "What if Dark King warned them about us? Let's vote on who we think should go. I think that Kayla should go. We can talk to her from our coms."

"Yeah, me too," Nick said. "She can transform into someone different and talk in a completely different accent."

"Same," Billy said. "She can just run out if she has trouble and transmit to us."

"What?" Kayla asked. "Come on, guys! What if something happens? I mean, I'm the youngest! I don't have experience with this sort of stuff!"

"Well, you've been outvoted," Ash said smugly.

"Fine!" Kayla grumbled and walked out of the spaceship.

"Can you hear me?" Ash asked through the coms.

"Loud and clear," Kayla said. "Wow!"

"What is it?" Ash asked.

Kayla was standing in tall grass, which went out for miles. She looked across the street, where she saw a building made from gold and decorated with diamonds and rubies.

"A palace!" Kayla said through the coms. "Maybe I can ask them for a hotel room!"

"Yeah, but make sure you are disguised," Ash said. "And talk in a southern accent."

Kayla transformed into an old woman with blue high heels, a white dress, and gray hair, then walked into the building.

CHAPTER TWENTY-FIVE:

THE HOTEL

Howdy," Kayla said, walking up to the front desk. "I'd like to know if this is a hotel."

She was inside what looked like a golden palace. Everything was gold except the floor, which was marble, and there was a vast diamond chandelier above her. There were two gold spiral staircases behind the gold front desk. A dark-skinned and blue-eyed woman stared back at them.

"*Elefesa?*" the woman asked. "*Wharto kel keste macte?*" She meant, "Sorry, what do you mean?" but she was talking in Karkarusian.

"Sorry, what?" Kayla asked.

"I know what she is saying!" Ash said through the coms.

"One second," Kayla told the woman. She went into a corner.

"I know what she is saying!" Ash said.

Kayla cocked her head to the side. "How?"

Ash slapped her forehead. "I heard it through the coms, and I had my translator on."

"Ohhhhhh," Kayla said, scratching her forehead.

"Just turn on your translator, and then you'll know what she is saying," Ash said.

"See, this is why I said you should have come," Kayla said. "I could have just transformed you, and you could have talked to her."

"Whatever just go back to her before we lose her, Kayla," Nick answered for Ash.

"Hey!" Ash exclaimed. "I was talking!"

"Can't I talk too?" Nick asked.

Kayla rolled her eyes and returned to the desk, turning her translator on.

"Hello," the woman said in Karkarusan. "How can I help you?"

"Could you please tell me if this is a hotel?" Kayla asked in the same language.

"Of course," the woman said. "You are in a hotel. I'm afraid this is not the best hotel, but it is decent."

Kayla's mouth dropped open.

"How much do I need to pay?" Kayla asked.

"50,000 gold coins," the woman said simply.

"50,000 gold coins?" Kayla exclaimed. "I don't have so much."

"You don't?" the woman asked, surprised. "Each person gets a googol gold coin as soon as they are born. You must be those intruders that my son Liam was talking about. Where are your evil siblings?"

Kayla looked terrified. "I have been here my whole life, and I don't have any evil siblings. But I didn't receive any coins when I was born."

"You are definitely an intruder," the woman said darkly. "Also, I don't have a son." Suddenly, Lucy was standing where the old woman had been. "Do you remember me?"

"Huh?" Kayla asked, trying to act surprised. "Who are you?"

"Oh, Kayla," Lucy sighed. "There is no need to act with me. My brother made sure that nobody could hide from me."

"Huh?" Kayla asked again. "I can't understand what you are saying."

"See," Lucy said, switching to English. "You have switched to English. I have turned all of your technology down. Remember, I am as powerful as my dear brother, but nobody cares about Dark Ness. They care about the king of darkness."

"Guys, I need help," Kayla said through the coms.

Nick immediately created a portal.

"Stay here," he told Billy. "Don't leave."

"But—"

"Bye," Nick said. He and Ash went through the portal and appeared in the hotel.

"Oh, hi, Ash!" Dark Ness said. "And Nick! Great to see you again! Did you bring Billy?"

"Where is your brother?" Nick asked Lucy, ignoring her questions.

"Oh him?" Lucy asked. "He has gone to rescue our father. And father will be angry. He has been left here for centuries."

"Well, why have you come to visit us?" Ash asked.

"Oh no," Lucy said. "You came to visit me. No, you're right. I expected you to come here, so I decided to meet you."

"But why?" Kayla asked.

"I have come here for Billy. We need him, you see, to help our father escape prison."

"I thought your brother was already there doing that," Ash said, confused.

"Well, he found a way to get into Zelosic, using the rock," Lucy said. "But he never thought about how he would get out."

"What does Billy have to do with that?" Kayla asked.

Just then, Billy entered the hotel.

"Billy! What are you doing here?" Nick exclaimed.

"You guys left me, and I wanted to see what was happening," Billy said.

"I told you to stay there!" Nick yelled.

Ash slapped her forehead.

"I have come for you, Billy!" Dark Ness said.

"Why me?" Billy asked.

"Well, you have two superpowers we need," Lucy said. "Your father actually works here in Karkarus. You are not from Earth. You are from Karkarus. Your father worked for the prison and wanted you to work there too. So, he allowed you to go to the prison and leave at will. That's how you will help us free my father. My brother is currently trapped in Zelosic because the Rock broke when he used it to get in. You must fix the rock for us so we can use it later and then bring back my father and brother."

Billy stared at Lucy. "What? My parents live on Earth! My father has no special abilities, and neither do I!"

"The people who you think are your parents are actually your adoptive parents," Lucy said. "And yes, you do have powers! You were moved to Earth at the age of ten, as Karkarus was becoming very dangerous. All memory of Karkarus was wiped out for your safety. But when you go into the subconscious part of your mind, you immediately remember everything as your memories are stored there."

"Well, I am not coming with you," Billy said firmly.

"Oh, but you are," Lucy said. She snapped her fingers, and Billy started to follow her. "Oh, yes. My dear brother told me to give you this." She gave Nick, Ash, and Kayla a letter and took Billy by the hand.

"Billy, Billy, wait!" Ash shouted. But Billy couldn't hear her. He couldn't hear anything. The only thing he could do was walk. Soon, Billy was out of sight.

"Now what?" Kayla asked.

"Come back to the rocket ship!" Ash exclaimed, opening the letter. She saw a chip inside it, which probably contained a video message "I found a video message from Dark King inside the letter."

They returned to their rocket and put the chip inside a player to play on a holographic screen.

"Hello, Nick, Ash, and Kayla," Dark King spoke from the holographic screen. "You must be wondering about the startling events that are happening. Billy leaving you, and Pegasus, Noah, Lucy, and Emma turning on you. Bet you didn't even think about what happened to Sam. But I can fix that. I can also tell you the answers to your biggest questions like, How did you get superpowers? How is Dark King so much more powerful than you are? This is something we are willing to give up. If you would like to know the answers to these questions and fix broken things, please meet me at the top of the Dark Tower in Deliwan at midnight on August 14th. Lucy, Noah, Emma, my father, and I will be there, and I will also tell you why my family and I decided to embrace the dark. Please come. Bye."

The video clip shut down.

CHAPTER TWENTY-SIX:
DELIWAN

"We are horrible people!" Nick exclaimed. "We never even thought about Sam!"

Ash looked at Nick strangely. "That is what you thought about after watching the video?!"

Kayla rolled her eyes. "So, are we going? August 14th, according to my calendar, is tomorrow, which means that we must go today at midnight."

"No," Nick said firmly. "It could be a trap."

"The key word in that is 'could,'" Ash said. "There is also a possibility that it isn't a trap."

"Okay," Nick sighed. "So, you guys think that they would give us all the answers we don't know, just like that, without doing anything for them or giving them anything, right?"

"Well, um, they might ask for something in return," Kayla stammered. "You never know."

"And what do you think that will be?" Nick asked sarcastically. "A handful of candy? A hundred dollars? They want us to join their team!"

"But we could just go and see," Ash protested. "We could go to that place well prepared."

"What doesn't make sense is why they want us there," Nick said. "If they want the rock, they can go to the place where it shattered and make Billy fix it. We wouldn't ever have known. So, why do they want us to be there?"

"True," Kayla said slowly. "But like Ash said, let's just go there prepared and see what Dark King wants instead of wondering."

"But he said midnight," Nick said. "It's only 6 a.m. What are we going to do till then?"

"We could search for the rock and try to get it," Ash suggested. "Maybe we could find a way to fix it and then use it to bring back all of the missing people."

"Yeah," Kayla agreed.

"Okay, fine," Nick grumbled. "But what will we do when we get the shattered pieces? And what if all of them aren't even there?"

"We'll figure it out then!" Ash exclaimed. "Right now, let's just go!"

"But where should we look?" Kayla asked.

"Um, how about we go and watch that memory that we tried to extract and look to see if there is a sign," Ash suggested. "If there is, we can go to that place."

"Okay," Nick and Kayla agreed.

They walked over to the infirmary and opened up the machine. Kayla and Nick went through the wires while Ash was using the device. He saw the saved video of Billy's memory and clicked on it.

"Okay," Ash said. "I found the memory." The video started to play. "Okay, so this place has a lot of fires." She looked around for a sign. "I can see it now; this place is called Deliwan."

"The exact place Dark King wants to meet us!" Nick said sarcastically. "How odd."

"Well, the good thing is that we can just stay in Deliwan all day and look for the rock since Dark King wants to meet us there, too," Kayla said quickly.

"Uh-huh," Ash agreed. "Let's get prepared."

"But I bet that Lucy and Billy have already found the rock and are already using it," Nick said.

"Well, they are just going to fix it," Ash said. "At least, that's what Lucy said. I don't know if they are going to bring it back to their hideout or not, but we'll figure that out later."

They put on their suits and masks, then gathered weapons, devices, and food.

"Let's go!" Kayla exclaimed, jumping into the air and levitating. "I am going to fly there!" She flew away.

"I am going to fly, too." Fire shot out of Nick's hands, and he flew away.

"And I can make myself a path made of ice," Ash said, pulling out her arms and shooting ice out, making a path in front of her. It was a giant ice hill that looked like one on a roller coaster. She let the ice move her around.

"Yippee!" Ash shouted. "This is fun!"

They flew in the air for a few hours until suddenly Nick shouted, "Guys! We're here!" He and Kayla slowly floated to the ground, and Ash slid down her ice ramp.

"Okay," Kayla said after they reached on grass. "This is totally not how I expected Deliwan to look."

Deliwan was a beautiful place. Flowers and nature were everywhere, children played on the streets, and everything was clean.

It was luxurious.

"Whoa," Ash gasped.

"I can't believe the Dark Tower could be here," Nick said.

"What if they were just trying to make us come here so we would be there when they hurt everyone?" Ash asked worriedly. "What if they were going to mind control us into hurting these people? What if—"

"What if, nothing," Kayla said, rolling her eyes.

"Okay," Nick said. "Now, how about we ask someone if there has been a fire somewhere?"

"Okay," they agreed.

Nick, Ash, and Kayla turned on their translators. Kayla transformed herself into a woman, and Nick and Ash into a man and a woman. They found a woman sitting on a bench.

"Hello," Kayla said with a precise Karkarusian accent. "Has there been a fire anywhere here? I heard that my friend died in a fire somewhere around here, and I want to see proof."

"I am not sure," the woman said. "I believe that there was a fire near Solowedge where the Dark Tower is, but nobody goes there." She shuddered. "It's a dark place, a very dark place."

"Could you please give me a map of Deliwan?" Kayla asked.

"A map?" the woman asked. "Everyone on Karkarus gets one map of the country they are living in. Why should I give up mine? And shouldn't you have one?"

"We would just like a copy," Kayla said. "We don't live here, you see. Could you make a copy of it?"

"Okay," the woman said. She took out the smallest possible chip, scanned another small chip with the chip, and the small chip was duplicated. "Here. You just press this button." She pressed a button on the side, and the map appeared, but it was digital. "And the map appears. Then, it just teleports you to the place that you tell it to teleport you to, but only if you want to teleport."

"Thank you," Kayla said. "Goodbye."

"You're welcome," the woman said, bowing. "Bye."

They left, hid behind a tree, and transformed back to normal.

"Okay, so in my opinion, that was the coolest map ever!" Kayla exclaimed.

"Yeah!" Ash exclaimed. "It was awesome."

"We have to use it!" Kayla shouted.

"Yeah, so let's go!" Nick exclaimed.

They opened up the map and looked at it.

"Okay," Nick said. "It says the Dark Tower is about a mile away, and it als—"

As soon as she heard that, Kayla immediately picked Nick and Ash up and sped to the Dark Tower.

"I was about to say we could have taken a train instead!" Nick said after they'd reached the area. He threw up.

On the corner, Ash was throwing up too.

"Yuck," Kayla said disgustedly.

Ash looked at the ground. "Guys … there are burn marks on the ground."

"Duh, there was a fire," Kayla said. "The real question is why, and where is the rock?"

"There are human burn marks," Nick said. "Ash, can you check whose burn marks they are?"

Ash took a sample and gave it to Nick.

"These are Billy's burn marks," Nick said.

They looked at each other, and Kayla burst into tears.

"Why?" Kayla asked. "Why, why, why?"

Nick and Ash started rubbing her on the back. They also felt tears pouring down.

"Guys!" Nick said after ten minutes. "If Billy is dead, that means …."

"Dark Star has escaped!" Ash continued, horrified.

CHAPTER TWENTY-SEVEN:
GOING BACK IN TIME

"So, they used him and then killed him," Ash repeated.

"Oh, come on!" Kayla said. "Can't that guy keep something when he's done? That's cruel even for him! And why, why did they have to kill Billy??"

"I-I don't know," Nick said sorrowfully.

"Guys!" Ash yelled. "Where is the Rock?"

They searched the ground. It was nowhere in sight.

"They must have taken it with them when they came back! "Kayla exclaimed.

"Now, what do we do?" Nick asked.

"I know we shouldn't, but I think I should time travel back to when the rock was just lying there," Ash said. "Then, we'll wait for Billy and Dark Star to appear, and then he'll throw Billy into the fire. We can wait for them to leave, pick up Billy, and get out of there!"

"Have you ever watched a movie about time travel?!" Kayla exclaimed. "Every time someone messes with time, things go wrong!"

"Well, we don't really have a choice here, do we?" Nick wondered. "If we don't get the Rock from Dark Star, the world will be destroyed anyway."

"I guess," Kayla said. "But we have to come too."

"Okay, sure," Ash chirped. "You can come."

"Yes!" Kayla exclaimed. "Let's go, let's go, let's go!"

"Okay," Ash said. "So, basically, I'm supposed to think about the time I want to go to and project that with my hands. Then a portal should open, and we should be there."

"Okay," Nick said. "So, just think about the time when a fire was here, recently, right before Dark Star came."

"Okay," Ash said. She closed her eyes. She thought. All about the Rock. She thought all about what would happen if they couldn't do this. The determination fueled her. She pushed all of it into her hands and shot it out. A portal appeared.

"Yippee!" Kayla exclaimed. "You did it!"

"Now, let's go!" Nick exclaimed.

"Yup," Ash said. "We've brought everything, right?"

"Yeah," Kayla said. "Before we left, I put a bunch of things in our pockets that I thought we'd need."

"Good," Nick said. "Let's go!"

They jumped into the portal. There was a lot of blue and purple everywhere. It was like they were in the middle of a tornado. It was exactly like how it felt when they had gone into the teleportation portal when they were going to Dark King's hideout. After a few seconds, they fell down exactly where they'd last been, except they were in a different time.

Kayla turned all of them into dogs.

"Really, Kayla," Nick barked. "A dog?"

"Yeah," Kayla barked. "A dog."

She ran over to the rock lying on the floor and picked it up with her mouth. She looked around to make sure Lucy wasn't watching; Lucy was just sitting there and looking at a Glic-Screen. She ran back to Nick and Ash. Kayla saw some rocks on the floor and turned them into bushes. She turned all of them back into humans.

Lucy heard the noise and looked around. She shrugged and turned back to her Glic-Screen.

"Now what?" Kayla asked quietly.

"We wait," Ash whispered.

They waited for a few minutes and saw a portal open. Dark King, Dark Star, and Billy walked out.

"We are done with you," Dark Star told Billy. Dark Star looked exactly like Dark King, except he had a stronger aura of power around him. His voice was more profound, and he sounded like he expected people to follow his orders no matter what. He nodded to Dark King, and Dark King made a fire and threw him in.

Billy screamed, a terrible, piercing scream that Nick, Ash, and Kayla knew they would never be able to forget. Kayla and Ash felt tears pouring down their cheeks, wishing they could help their friend right then but knowing they couldn't.

"WHERE IS THE ROCK?!" Dark Star howled. "DARK NESS, WHERE HAVE YOU PUT IT?"

"Um, it should be right there," Dark Ness said, coming over to Dark Star. She looked around. "Wait a second, where did it go??"

"NOOOOO!!!" Dark Star yelled. Everything exploded around them. He looked at Dark Ness. "YOU SHALL BE PUNISHED FOR YOUR BEHAVIOR!!"

"Please, father, don't do this to me!" Dark Ness pleaded.

Dark Star walked away in disgust. Dark King followed him. Dark Ness ran up to them and continued begging.

Soon, they were out of sight.

"Okay, Nick, go quick!" Ash shouted.

Nick quickly ran and picked up Billy. Then he went back to join his sisters.

"Good," Kayla said. "Now, let's go back."

Ash did precisely what she had done before, and the portal opened. They jumped through. But this time, they were only in the portal for a millisecond until they reached when they had started. They saw the portal close.

"Okay, so we're at the right time, right?" Nick asked. All of the trees were burned, but that was the only difference.

"Yup," Ash said. "We are. I just hope we didn't change too much."

"Yeah," Kayla agreed. "Now we need medical assistance! Nick! Teleport us!"

Nick made a portal into the rocket's infirmary, and Kayla put Billy on the bed.

Nick checked his pulse. "He's alive, but barely. Ash, I need your help."

"Okay," Ash said.

Kayla sat outside the infirmary for a while.

Soon, Nick and Ash came out with a smile.

"He's back," they beamed.

CHAPTER TWENTY-EIGHT:

THE FIGHT

"Wait," Kayla said. "He's alive and not controlled anymore?"

"Yup," Ash said happily. "You can come and see him."

Kayla went into the infirmary to see Billy. Meanwhile, Nick and Ash sat in front of the ship and started talking.

"Why did they put Billy in the fire?" Ash asked. "I mean, even though they said they didn't have any more use for him, they knew that he was useful. He would have been a good ally."

"What if they put Billy in a fake fire just so that when we take him back to the spaceship to heal him, he will have access to us!" Nick exclaimed. "Maybe they are still controlling him and trying to take our powers away! If he does that, we will die because to take away our powers, he will have to suck all the blood out of us! And we will be dead! Dark Star won't want us to join his team anymore because we will not have powers and not be of any use to him. They already know they won't be able to convince us, which is why they are doing this!"

"Since Kayla's in the room with him, he will take the stone from her and kill her!" Ash yelled.

They rushed into the room and saw Kayla on the floor.

Nick ran to her and checked her pulse. "She's alive but barely holding on," he said. "Her heart is pumping like crazy to recover all the blood she has lost. But her heart can't take this much pressure!"

Ash looked at the bed. Billy had escaped.

Nick looked up at Ash. He was struggling, trying to pick Kayla up.

"A little help please?" he asked Ash.

Ash stepped forward and helped Nick.

"I'll have to do a few stitches," Nick said. "She won't feel them, and it won't hurt her."

"I have to go," Ash said, and she rushed out the door.

She walked down the hallway of the rocket ship. It was dark, and there was a smoky smell. Suddenly, she heard a growling noise.

"Come out, come out, wherever you are," Sad Ness growled.

Ash followed the noise to a bedroom. She rushed in, and the door closed behind her. She could feel sweat dripping down her neck.

"What kind of superhero are you?" Sad Ness asked. "You can't even save your sister. How will you save the world?"

Sad Ness looked like Billy, except his eyes were completely black.

"Don't talk about Kayla like that!" Ash yelled.

Sad Ness leaped forward, aiming for Ash with a sword, but Ash ran to the corner of the room.

She focused on her powers and started making icicles. She threw one at Sad Ness, and he dodged. The second one he also avoided. For the third one, she focused on his feet, aimed harder, and struck them.

Sad Ness's feet started to turn to ice, and he struggled to balance. He fell down on the floor, then shot poison from his hands. Ash dodged it. She continued shooting ice, but Sad Ness avoided all of them. Then he started hitting her with his own icicles. Ash dodged most of them, but one pierced her arm.

"Ow," Ash muttered. The pain was horrible. She felt like she was about to faint.

"Ha ha ha ha ha," Sad Ness laughed. "You can't beat me! I am—"

But he couldn't finish that sentence because Ash shot him in the arm with an icicle. He couldn't bear the pain and fainted.

"Yay!" Ash exclaimed. She pulled out the icicle from her arm. "Ow!" Her arm started to heal because of her healing power, and soon the mark was almost gone. The pain began to fade. She walked out of the room carrying Billy and went back into the infirmary. There she saw Kayla sitting up. "Kayla!" she exclaimed. "You're up!"

"Yup," Kayla said happily. "Nick gave me a transfusion from the blood supply here, and since I have fast healing power, I am fine."

"I'm so glad!" Ash exclaimed. "Well, I just defeated Sad Ness, so we'll keep him in our prison. We can try the trigger again."

"Okay," Kayla said. "How about you go do that, Nick? I want to talk to Ash for a moment."

"Sure," Nick said and left, carrying Billy.

"Okay, Ash," Kayla said. "I want to tell you what happened."

"Okay," Ash said. "But why aren't you telling Nick?"

"He wouldn't want to wake up Billy then," Kayla said. "Billy, umm … Sad Ness told me how to make the trap. Remember, in my notes, I mentioned that the only way to beat Dark Star is to make a trap using the rock? I said I would give him something in return, which I didn't, which is one of the reasons why he tried to kill me. Anyway, tell Nick to wake Billy up, okay?"

"Hold on, why me?" Ash asked.

"Because I don't feel like convincing someone or arguing right now," Kayla answered, leaning back on her cot. "I've just had a ton of blood sucked out of me. I need to, y'know, relax."

"Fine!" Ash grumbled. She left the room and came back a few minutes later. "Nick is waking Billy up right now."

"How did it go?" Kayla asked.

"Great!" Ash grumbled sarcastically. "Nick was kind and helpful and listened to me as soon as I asked!"

"What?" Kayla asked. "He's our friend!"

"Whatever!" Ash grumbled. "But he did agree at the end."

"So," Kayla said. "We need to transfer a little bit of all of our powers into the rock, and then we need to show the rock a picture of our idea. After that, we need to scan the room with the rock, and our idea will just appear."

"Okay," Ash said. "Good."

"Yeah," Kayla said.

"Wait, instead of us going to the Dark Tower, how about we call them here?" Ash asked. "I can't believe that it's only four o'clock. We still have eight hours left."

"Okay," Kayla said slowly. "But how will we tell them?"

"Just go to the hotel again," Ash said. "Nick and I will take the blueprint and make the trap. You can tell Dark Ness."

"Sure," Kayla replied. "But first, let's check on Nick. I feel fine already."

"How about I just call Nick?" Ash suggested.

"Okay, works too," Kayla said.

"Nick, come here!" Ash ordered through the coms.

"Coming!" Nick said. He appeared through the doorway with Billy at his side. "Billy is fixed!"

"Yup," Billy said. "I'm fixed."

They opened up the machine and put it on Billy. Everything seemed to be okay.

"Billy!" Kayla exclaimed. "You're okay!"

"Yup!" he chirped.

"I'm just so glad you are okay," Kayla said. She started crying.

Then Billy started crying.

"Okay, this is getting way too emotional," Nick said. Nick and Ash started patting Kayla and Billy on the back.

"Anyways, let's get to work!" Ash exclaimed.

"Hold on, what do you mean?" Billy asked.

"Oh yeah, we didn't tell you!" Kayla realized.

"When you were Sad Ness, you told Kayla how to make the trap," Nick explained. "Now, let's build the trap!"

"Yeah!" Ash exclaimed. "First, let's fix the rock, then Billy and I can draw a picture of how the trap is supposed to look, and Nick and Kayla can make the letter. Then Nick can help Billy and me, and we can get all the supplies while Kayla delivers the letter to Sad Ness."

"Yeah, about that. Billy can't do it," Kayla said.

Ash stepped on Kayla's foot. "Don't!"

Kayla ignored Ash and went on. "Nick said something to me through the coms; Ash knows too, and he's right; it is too dangerous to have Billy around."

"What?" Billy asked sadly. "You don't want me around?"

"It's not that we don't want you around; it is that you are just too dangerous," Nick said. "Who knows when you will turn into Sad Ness? Kayla and Ash almost died today because of you! Sorry, Billy, but you have to go."

"Yeah, we'll drop you off in a hotel, and you will stay there till this is all over," Ash said.

"But after this is over, you can help us with our next mission!" Kayla exclaimed.

"Yup," Nick said. "You can."

CHAPTER TWENTY-NINE:

DELIVERING THE MESSAGE

They dropped Billy off. Nick and Ash had taken out a massive piece of paper for their blueprint of the trap. They were deciding what to draw, while Kayla had just written a letter that said,

Hello, Dark Star,

Instead of meeting you at the Dark Tower, we have decided to meet in our spaceship simultaneously. We will know you are afraid of us if you don't come.

Our coordinates are 100, 25 in the city of Marco.

From: The Tech Superheroes

Nick and Ash were drawing on the paper. Meanwhile, Kayla walked out of the ship and headed toward the hotel across the street, hoping that Dark Ness was still there. Once she got there, she walked up to the shimmering gold desk.

"Hello?" Kayla asked in English.

Lucy was behind the counter, using the same disguise as before. She squinted at Kayla and shrugged.

"Um, why can't you understand me?" Kayla asked. "Aren't you Lucy?"

Lucy just shrugged again.

"Hello?" Kayla asked, waving her hands in front of Lucy's face.

After she still didn't answer, Kayla gave up and pressed the button on the side of her suit that translated everything she said to Karkrasian.

"Hello," Kayla repeated.

"Ah, hi!" Lucy replied.

"Okay, give it up! I know it's you, Lucy. So just switch into your Lucy disguise."

"I have no idea who you're talking about!" Lucy said, still confused.

"Whatever, just give this note to Dark Star, okay?" Kayla put the note on the desk, turned around, and started to walk away.

"Dark Star!!??" Lucy said furiously.

Kayla quickly whipped around. "Huh?"

"How dare you talk about him?" Lucy asked.

"Okay, what is wrong with him? I mean, I know he's evil and stuff, but so are you! First Thea gets mad, now you. And besides, you are his child!"

"I am not his child! Do not talk about Thea or anyone that is related to him!"

Lucy quickly transformed into one of the zombie ghost robots.

"Ahhh!" Kayla squealed.

"I used to be the leader of my kind until that Dark Star kicked me out and left me to die! All of them did!"

"Um, okay," Kayla said, shaking.

"Take me to Dark Star!" The angry ghost robot yelled, turning into a human warrior. He wore a military uniform and jet-black hair and pulled a dagger out of his green vest.

Kayla used telekinesis to take the dagger from his hands.

"How did you get that?" He sputtered.

Kayla smirked and turned into a fighting pose.

A new dagger appeared in the warrior's hand, and he charged at Kayla. She flicked it out of his hand, making it land on her hand, and aimed it toward him.

Kayla made sure it didn't touch him, but it almost did. The warrior looked really, really mad. He did a flip and appeared next to Kayla, who used her super-speed to run away, and then she punched the warrior quickly three times. A dagger appeared in the warrior's hand. He pushed it toward Kayla, but using her super speed, she dodged it. The warrior transformed into a vast cheetah that started chasing her around with a dagger in its mouth. Kayla used her super speed to rush away and telekinesis to remove the blade from the cheetah's mouth. She aimed it toward the cheetah's leg. He howled as it hit his leg, then used his teeth to pull the dagger out. Then he charged again. Kayla used her super speed and bit the cheetah, which howled and turned back into the human warrior. Kayla pinned him to the ground.

"Okay, okay," the warrior said. "I'll stop fighting you; just let me go!"

Kayla lifted her arms and started to walk away.

"What do you want?" the warrior asked.

"All I wanted was for you to deliver this letter to Dark Star, but you don't like him, so I can't do anything about that." Kayla sighed. "I thought that you were Lucy, also known as Dark Ness, so I asked you to give the note to him."

"I can handle that," a familiar voice behind them said.

Kayla turned around. "Oh, hi, Lucy."

"Just give me the note!" She snatched it out of Kayla's hand and disappeared.

"Well, that was rude," Kayla said. "She didn't even say hi or bye. Well, I guess that's the behavior of all bad guys. I don't like them." She turned around to look at the warrior. "Well, I don't like you, so I will not say bye!" She turned away and walked out of the hotel and into their spaceship.

Kayla joined Ash and Nick in a massive room with green and red walls. The only furniture in that room was a round, black marble table. It was the room where they were going to set the trap because the spaceship's other rooms were too small. Nick and Ash had been deciding what to put in it.

"Hey, Kayla," Ash said. "We finished making the drawing of the trap."

"Okay, guys," Nick said. "Let's transfer!"

"Transfer?" Kayla asked.

"Into the rock," Nick said.

"Oh yeah."

They touched the rock, but nothing happened.

"Seriously?" Nick complained.

Suddenly the room started to glow. A disco light appeared out of nowhere.

"Whoa, what's going on?" Ash asked.

"I have no idea," Kayla said.

"Hi!" The rock said, suddenly gaining eyes, a mouth, a nose, and ears. "My name is Willy? How's it going?"

Nick, Ash, and Kayla screamed. "Ahhhhhhhhhh!"

CHAPTER THIRTY:

THE ROCK

"Who are you, what are you doing, and how are you alive?!" Nick yelled.

"Also, what kind of a name is Willy?" Kayla said.

"That rhymes with Billy!" Ash exclaimed. "You guys could be best friends!"

"Yeah, Billy and Willy!" Kayla exclaimed.

"Guys, we're getting off-topic," Nick said.

"Oh, sorry," Ash replied.

"My name is Willy, and I am the rock of creation," Willy explained. "I have come alive because you guys put your powers into me. I am here to be your assistant! What are you doing at 5:00? We could have a nice tea and get to know each other!"

"Um, yeah, no," Kayla said.

"We have an appointment with Dark Star," Ash said. "Y'know, WE CAN DIE!"

"I'm so sorry," Willy said. "What can I do to help? Maybe you guys can give me all your stuff when you are gone. Here's a paper. Write that down so that I am not charged for stealing stuff."

"For the last time, you. Are. A. Rock!" Nick's face was steaming red.

"No? Okay, how about we sit down, and you tell me all your problems! Have you been missing your old teachers and friends? Actually, probably not. Is Dark Star being a meanie? Do the Techie Supers want a huggie? Let me help you get rid of your problems!" Willy sprouted hands and curved them in a hugging position.

"Oh, one of our problems will disappear, alright!" Kayla charged at the rock.

Ash moved the rock away, and Kayla banged into a wall.

"OWWW!" Kayla cried. "Why did you do that?"

"Guys," Nick whispered to them, turning around and glancing at the rock. "You're embarrassing me!"

"Oh, I'm sorry! Does little Nicky want a huggie?" Ash teased.

"Stop it," Nick whined.

"Awwww," Kayla said. "And you think we're embarrassing you!"

Nick scoffed and crossed his arms, turning back to the rock. "Let's get back to business here."

"Why didn't it work?" he asked. "This power thingy was supposed to make a huge trap."

"Well…maybe this rock, or Willy, is the key to helping us make the trap," Ash guessed.

"Willy? The secretary who wants to have tea with us?" Kayla asked. "The rock who asked if we wanted a huggie?"

"Yes, him!" Ash exclaimed.

"How do we get him to make the trap?" Nick asked. "We don't even know where he came from!"

"Um, you guys are the ones who brought me here!" Willy exclaimed. "Your 'power thingy' didn't work because you have not to beat that person in battle yet! Well, you've got to beat most of those people in battle. So, who's the lucky guy? I doubt it's the bully, Dark Star. He wouldn't have gotten into a war with children."

"Well, you're wrong. It *is* Dark Star and his children," Kayla answered.

Willy winced, suddenly getting eyebrows. "Oh. Well, you are doomed. Might as well say goodbye to the world after all. It's been nice knowing you. I guess our te-"

"We are not giving up," Ash said. "You are going to help us. Dark Star and his children will be here by midnight. We need to prepare for war! Tell us what to do, little rocky. You were, after all, created by Dark Star himself."

"Well, first of all, Dark Star can't even know about this war you guys are planning. He hates surprises. If he is surprised, he'll be so mad, he won't be able to fight his best!"

Kayla put down the letter she was writing. "Oops, sorry!"

"Anyways, moving on. You guys need to be 100% ready. Dark Star has a big army and is very powerful. He's got moves." Willy sprouted legs and started rocking back and forth with his hands in fists.

"As if we didn't know that already!" Nick but in.

"Next, you guys need to practice your powers. You guys must be experts at using each and every one of them. Also, you guys need to get signature moves. That would be cool." The rock did a flying high side kick, then karate chopped the air. "Everyone will have a different job in preparing for this war. Ash, you go and get the supplies and weapons-"

"Hold on," Kayla interrupted. "We have weapons?"

"Yes, and if you want to be able to use them, please stop interrupting!" Nick reprimanded.

"Fine, sorry!" Kayla muttered.

"As I was saying. Ash, go and get the weapons. Kayla, get the suits and first aid kits ready. And Nick, you go and get the battlegrounds ready. Don't be afraid to put in traps. Remember, since this is our ground, and since Dark Star doesn't even know about the war, we have an advantage."

"Wait a second," Ash said.

"Yes?" Willy answered, annoyed.

"If Dark Star doesn't even know about the war or the trap, he won't bring his soldiers or weapons," Ash said. "Why do we have to prepare so much?"

"Well, first of all, Dark Star carries his weapons around everywhere. Second, if he didn't have his weapons, he could still make them appear out of thin air. Third, if he didn't have his weapons and couldn't do that, he would make his soldiers appear out of thin air. Anyways, he is probably going to bring his children. He knows we are planning something, and he'll be suspicious because of that."

"Okay, thanks," Ash said.

"Yeah, whatever. After you have everything ready, we will have a *very* intense battle session. We won't do *too* much because we don't want you to get exhausted, blah, blah, blah. Any questions?"

"Yeah, one thing. I didn't get the blah blah blah part," Kayla said.

"Kayla!" Nick yelled. "Enough goofing around! We have a war to prepare for! Now, like Willy said, get to work!"

"Fine, but jeez! You don't have to yell!"

Everyone left to go get the supplies. Ash headed to the weapons room, Nick headed outside, and Kayla went to the med room and the living quarters. Willy was lying on the table. "Um, guys! What about me?" Unfortunately, everyone left, and nobody really wanted to bring him along.

Willy continued to yell. "HELP ME! DON'T LEAVE ME TO DIE! I HAVE A LIFE TOO, Y'KNOW!"

"Hey Willy, keep it down, will you?" Nick yelled.

"Wai-bu-wh-" Willy stammered.

"That's better, thanks," Nick said.

* *

Kayla was in the med room.

"Now, where could the first aid kits be?" Kayle muttered to herself. She quickly used her superspeed and raced around the area, finding it in under a millisecond.

"Phew, that took a while," Kayla said. "1 millisecond. Yikes. I better practice my super speed. I think I might be losing my powers! Anywho, off to get the suits!"

She raced to the living quarters and ran inside the closets. She picked up the newest version of their suits with the first aid kits and ran back to the control room.

* *

Ash was in the weapon room. "Now, what weapons would we need?"

The weapons room had old silver walls and bronze metal shelves everywhere. There was almost every weapon you can imagine stacked everywhere. There were many different versions of Raydes; high energy ones, ones that blasted lasers, lower energy ones for training, long one's short ones. There were shields; big shields, small shields, throwing frisbee shields. There were many laser guns as well; Gedlastic 2.0 for far away shooting, Gedlastic 1.0 for close-up shooting, Gedlastic 3.0 for exploding areas, and finally the Gedlastic 4.0, for – 360 degrees Fahrenheit lasers. There were also spears, hand-thrown javelins, daggers, crossbows, and bows and arrows, each with giant, small, laser shooting, electricity, and poison versions.

"So we will need the Gedlastic 1.0, 2.0; I don't feel like blowing anything up today, so not the other Gedlastics. We will need high-energy long Raydes, throwing frisbee shields, big shields, crossbows, poison bow and arrows, electric daggers, electric spears, and electric javelins."

Ash picked up the stuff. She groaned. "Wow, this is heavy; I should have had Nick and Kayla help me."

She slowly walked back to the control room.

* *

Nick was outside on the 'battlefield.' The 'battlefield' would be just outside the ship. As soon as he walked outside, all he could see was green.

He sighed. "I guess I have to chop all of this grass." He slowly started plucking the grass, one by one.

"Maybe they have a machine," Nick said to himself after plucking his 100th one. "I sure hope so. I am *exhausted* already, and I am barely 1/100 of the way there.

He went into the nearest room from the door that led outside. There he found a vast lawn mower. "How did I not know that we had this?"

He started to snip the grass. *"Ugh,"* he thought. *"This will take a long time."*

He stopped suddenly, making the machine roll over. "Oww," he mumbled. He got up and threw the machine away. "Wait a second. I have superpowers. What am I doing all this work for?" He slapped his forehead.

Nick closed his eyes and focused on his whole body turning into fire. When he opened his eyes, he saw that his body was blazing. His eyes widened, and his natural instincts told him to put the fire out, but he used all his willpower to not listen. He took a deep breath and rolled up into a ball. Then, he started rolling around like a ball, super-fast, on fire, all around the grass. Most of the grass except the bottom turned to ashes and blew into the air.

He uncurled himself, wiped his hands on each other, and stood up. "Well, now it is time to get started with the traps and the setup."

Nick went to get more supplies. He went into the same room as before and grabbed things like rope and water. He went to large patches of grass and made portals leading to space and portals leading to nowhere. Then he tied ropes in other parts of the ground to trap their enemy. Lastly, he grabbed the water and mixed it with the dirt making it *very* slippery mud.

"Well, looks like my work here is done!" Nick announced to himself 30 minutes later.

He headed back to the control room.

Inside, he saw Kayla talking to Willy.

No, not talking.

Fighting.

CHAPTER THIRTY-ONE:
PREPARING FOR WAR

"Whoa, whoa, whoa, what's going on here?" Nick asked. "And where is Ash?"

Kayla turned around. Her face was filled with sweat. "Well, I finished my work early, so I came back. Then, I just said something about Willy not doing anything and laughed like I was making a joke. Then Willy started giving me this whole lecture about why I shouldn't be like myself, an-"

"That's not what I said!" Willy exclaimed. "I just said that sometimes making jokes is not a good thing!

"Well, making jokes is my thing!" Kayla exclaimed. "Are you saying tha-"

"Well, whatever the reason, you two shouldn't be fighting!" Nick exclaimed. We have bigger enemies to worry about. Like Dark Star and his children. Now tell me, where is Ash??"

"Right here!" Ash said as she fell to the floor. "So heavy!"

Nick and Kayla went to help Ash pick up the weapons.

"Time to get your suits and weapons ready! It is almost midnight!" Willy reminded them.

Nick, Ash, and Kayla all ran to their individual rooms to change and get ready. Once their suits were on, they returned to the control room and decided on weapons.

"Each of us should take a rayde and 3 other weapons," Kayla said.

They discussed the weapons and decided who would take what.

Nick took the Gedlastic 1.0, a high-energy rayde, a crossbow, and an electric spear.

Ash took a high-energy rayde, the big shield, the poison bow and arrow, and the electric daggers.

Kayla took the Gedlastic 2.0, a high-energy rayde, the frisbee throwing shields, and the hand-thrown electric javelins.

"Looks like we are all ready to go!" Ash exclaimed.

"I think I heard Dark Star and his children outside," Will says. "You guys should get going."

"Okay, guys, now is our chance to stop them," Nick said. "Remember, no matter what happens, we're in this together. Even if you fall or want to quit, just remember that what you are doing is for the greater good. I love you guys!" Nick's voice squeaked at the end, and he covered his face and looked away.

"We love you too!" Ash and Kayla replied, starting to cry.

They all go in for a hug.

"Oh my god, can you guys be any sappier? A war is going on outside, and you guys are crying and hugging?" Willy interrupted.

They broke out of their hug.

Kayla glared at Willy. "You spoiled a critical family moment! Do you know how rare this sort of stuff happens? Shame on you, Willy! Shame. On. You!"

"Yeah, yeah, whatever," Willy grumbled. "What's the plan?"

"Basically, the three of us will stand close to each other in a triangular shape, facing the bad guys an-"

"Why a triangle?" Ash interrupted.

"Don't interrupt me!" Nick replied. "Maybe you will find out! So, as I was saying, after that, do what your instincts tell you!"

"Areyoukiddingme? That'sthebestyoucando?" Ashraisesher eyebrows. "Just go along with it!" Nick said. "And if I tell you to do something during the war, please listen!"

"No promises, Buddy," Kayla said.

"Well, let's head out to war!" Ash yelled.

And they walked out and into the battlefield.

CHAPTER THIRTY-TWO:

THE WAR PART I

"Hello, nephew and nieces," Dark Star growled.

They stood in the middle of the battlefield that Nick had made.

"'Sup, uncle," Kayla growled in the same manner. She turned around and looked at Nick and Ash. "Good mimicking?"

"I am so sorry about her. I have no idea what happened," Ash apologized, ignoring Kayla.

"ENOUGH!" Dark Star yelled.

Nick, Ash, and Kayla cowered.

"Sorry," Kayla squeaked.

"SORRY DOESN'T FIX WHAT YOU DID!" Dark Star countered.

"What did we do?" Ash asked, crossing her arms.

"UM… YOU TALKED," Dark Star replied. "Your voices disturb my aura."

"What aura?" Nick wondered. "Now you are just making things up."

"Can we just start whatever we are doing already? I am late for a pilates class!" Dark King complained.

"What?" Ash squinted her eyebrows.

"You embarrass me," Dark Star told Dark King.

"Yeah, yeah, whatever," Dark King muttered.

"So, how's it going?" Kayla asked.

"JUST TELL ME WHAT YOU WANT!" Dark Star yelled.

"This," Nick said. He raised his hand and shot an inferno of fire right onto Dark Star's body.

"Huh?" Dark Star asked.

When Dark Star was trying to figure out what was going on, Ash sneaked up behind him and absorbed his powers.

"Whoa, I feel dizzy," Ash muttered, quietly fainting.

Nick caught her. "Ash, wake up."

Ash slowly opened her eyes. "Huh?"

"Come on, chop-chop, you've gotta get up," Nick said. "We've got a battle to fight!"

"Oh yeah, right." Ash slowly stood up, and she curled her fists. "I'm ready."

Dark Star turned pale. "What in the world is going on?" he exclaimed. He tried to run away. "Children, I think these kids just took away my powers! Help me!"

"Not on my watch," Kayla muttered as she super-speeded towards Dark Star with a rope.

She quickly tied him up, picked him up, and ran away.

"I'm going after her," Dark Chief yelled. "You guys fight the other kids!"

"On it," some sibling said.

Dark Chief chased after Kayla.

"Whoops," Kayla muttered. "I didn't realize that she had super speed too…"

"I'm coming for you!" Dark Chief yelled. She started to slowly catch up to Kayla.

Kayla raced around. "Well, it's time to use my advantage!"

She raced around the battlefield. "Where could Nick have put the traps? Eh, I'll just figure it out as it comes."

"Kayla! Drop Dark Star off in one of the traps!" Ash yelled.

"Yeah, I know; I was going to do that anyway!" "What? What trap?!" Dark Star asked.

"You'll see," Kayla smirked.

Kayla saw a small circular tornado thing going into the ground. It had black stuff on the bottom.

Kayla dropped Dark Star in the portal. "Let me out of this!" he yelled as the portal closed.

Kayla just smirked and super speeded away.

* *

"We're ready for you," Nick said. "Come on, attack us! We got this! Am I right, Ash?"

"Uh-huh!" Ash replied. "You take those two. I'll do these two."

"What about the others?" Nick asked.

"I'll take the rest!" Kayla said, coming back. She shot one of the siblings with her electric javelin, who promptly fell. "See, I got this!"

Ash gave a sigh of relief as she and Nick faced their opponents.

Ash took on Dark King and Dark Chief. Nick took on Dark Ness and Dark Ruler.

Ash ducked as Dark King blasted her with fire. She did a somersault backward and blasted both of them with ice. Dark Chief shot a laser at Ash. Ash slowed down time and made a clear ice sculpture in the shape of a mirror. As soon as she slowed down time, the laser reflected off the glass and hit Dark Chief. She fell to the floor and clutched her stomach.

"I guess it's just you and me now," Ash said to Dark King.

"You know that Dark Chief and I are immortal, right," Dark King reminded Ash.

"I know, but you will already be down when Dark Chief recovers."

Dark King scoffed. "Yeah, right. Bring it on."

Ash slid under Dark King's legs and jumped up on the other side. She brought out an electric dagger in one hand and a shield in the other.

"Aww, you brought out your toys," Dark King said in a baby voice.

Ash rolled her eyes. "You won't be laughing when I beat you."

Dark King opened up a portal and pulled Ash into it. Ash looked around; there were miles and miles of sand and sand dunes around her.

"Where did you take me," Ash asked.

"Isn't it obvious? The Sahara Desert."

"But why-" Ash started. That is when she realized. Here, her ice would melt.

"For someone with section intelligence, you aren't very smart," Dark Star pointed out."

"Well, I'll never be as smart as you!" Ash said sarcastically.

Dark King looked confused. "Really?"

Ash rolled her eyes. "No! Of course not!"

Dark King controlled the dirt from the ground and levitated it up in the air, creating a sand vortex around Ash. The sand burned in Ash's eyes. She fell onto the floor and tried to shield herself from the storm. She created an ice shield and hid behind it. But the shield kept melting.

"I'm gonna have to make a new shield every few seconds," Ash muttered to herself.

She formed a new shield around her and kept making one every time it melted.

Suddenly, she felt a tug in her chest and a cold hand on her shoulder. Ash looked around but couldn't see Dark King. She felt a cold touch on her shoulder.

Uh oh, she thought. Ash turned around and saw Dark King's hand on her shoulder. She started to feel a numbing sensation and watched as white clumps of light floated out of her chest and into Dark King.

"What did you do to me?" Ash yelled.

"I just absorbed all your powers," Dark King said with a smirk. "Do you admit that you have lost?"

"Oh no," Ash said. "See, that is something you don't know about me." She grabbed her Rayde and shield. "I will never give up."

She charged at Dark King in the vortex, not caring that the sand was going into her eyes.

Dark King's eyes widened. He created a portal back to where the battle was happening.

"Are you scared now?" Ash asked with a smirk. "You've come back to the main battlefield. Do you want to fight against me with your siblings?"

"What, no," Dark King said. "It's just... well, it's not fair that you don't have powers."

"Then give me them back!" Ash shouted.

"Well, I wouldn't want to do that now, would I?" Dark King smirked. "Let's not do this battle with powers. Let's do it based on fighting capability." He drew out a long rayde and an electric spear.

"Fine." Ash had no fear in her eyes. She charged at Dark King with all her might.

Dark King blocked it with his Rayde. He swiped at Ash's legs with his electric dagger. Ash wasn't fast enough and got electrocuted.

"Ha," Dark King said as Ash trembled on the ground. "See? There was no way you could beat me!"

Ash gritted her teeth. "It's too early to tell that." She pulled out her electric dagger with all her force and swiped at Dark King's feet. Dark King fell to the ground and started to tremble.

"If I'm going down, you're coming with me," Ash said as her vision started to blur.

Then, everything went black.

CHAPTER THIRTY-THREE:

THE WAR PART II

Nick curved his fists and jumped into an attack position. "Come on. Attack me!"

"That's cute," Dark Ness said with a smirk. "But we both know that I can beat you."

"Uh, what about me?" Dark Ruler asked.

"Yeah, yeah, you too," Dark Ness said, with a flap of her arm.

"You do know that we are immortal, right?" Dark Ruler asked.

"Wait, what?" Nick asked. *I must have forgotten*, he thought. *Whoops*. "Oh, yeah, that. Pffff. I totally knew that." "And how do you expect to beat us?" Dark Ness asked.

"Uh, well, I'm going to try!" Nick yelled. Immediately he shot out fire and aimed it at Dark Ruler.

Dark Ruler promptly put up a force field. The fire disintegrated. "Nice try. But everything you aim at us will either disintegrate or rebound."

"Well, maybe not everything...." Nick smirked. He shot fire and then quickly made a teleportation portal leading inside the force field that

Dark Ruler had earlier made. The fire flamed. When it calmed down, Dark Ruler's face looked burned.

Unfortunately, it started to heal.

"We can play tricks too," Dark Ness said. Slowly, a vine emerged from the ground and started to wrap around Nick.

"Ahhh!" Nick yelled. He started to burn the vine. It turned into ashes.

"You know what?" Nick said. "This is it. This is enough of going easy on you guys. Now, I'm going full-on. All my strength."

"Sure," Dark Ruler said. "We're ready."

"Fine." Nick gathered a lot of fire in his hand. He shot it out and into a portal, which went inside the force field.

Dark Ness must have expected that because she surrounded herself and Dark Ruler with water. Dark Ruler then opened the force field and shot out a lightning bolt. Nick did a backflip and came back on the ground. He then turned into a ball and rolled at 300 MPH towards Dark Ness and Dark Ruler.

Dark Ruler started to make a force field, but he was too late. Nick had rolled right in.

"Well, I guess there's no point in having a force field now then, is there?" Dark Ruler asked. "Let's do this without the force field."

"Good," Nick said.

He once again turned into a ball and started chasing Dark Ness and Dark Ruler. Dark Ness started making tall vines to stop Nick, but it didn't stop him. Nick rolled right through them. She started shooting him with poison. But she missed every time since Nick was going too fast.

Nick started going in circles since he was going too far.

"Now I'm going to try something I have only done once before," Nick muttered. "Three, two, one." He concentrated, and he went on fire. Literally, the ball that he turned into was on fire. He burned everything that he rolled over, and fire surrounded them. He started to narrow his circle, slowly by slowly.

"Fine, well, we're going to have to take this up a notch," Dark Ruler said. He concentrated and started to raise Nick.

"HEY!" Nick yelled. He turned back to normal. He struggled in the air and tried to get free, but he couldn't do anything.

Dark Ruler nodded to Dark Ness. Dark Ness nodded back and made a portal that led to space.

"WHAT? YOU CAN'T DO THIS TO ME! I HAVEN'T DONE ANYTHING WRONG! I-"

Suddenly, Nick dropped to the ground, and, "Ow," he groaned. "Thank you so much! I really owe you, the person who helped me!"

"You owe me a lot," Kayla replied.

Nick looked up. There was Kayla with her hand raised, lifting up Dark Ruler and Dark Ness.

"Whoa," Nick said. "You already defeated all the other siblings?"

"Yeah," Kayla said. "Pfff, it was easy. Those people don't know how to fight."

"Oh, okay," Nick said.

Suddenly, Kayla froze. Her eyes were wide open. She fell face-first onto the ground.

"Kayla!" Nick yelled. He went to her and picked her up. She didn't move. Nick checked her pulse. It was faster than usual.

"YOU-" Nick yelled. "HOW DARE YOU??" Nick's entire body went on fire. He started walking towards Dark Ruler and Dark Ness, who had dropped back to the ground.

Dark Ness started shooting poison at Nick, but Nick just turned his hands into rocks and flicked them away.

For just a brief second, Nick saw fear in her eyes. He grinned evilly.

"I guess I'm not the only scared one around here, huh?" Nick said.

"What do you mean? Dark Ness asked, freezing in place.

"I mean, that I know that you are scared right now. Of me, Ash, Kayla, and us beating you."

"Beating us?" she scoffed. "How could you ever beat us? We are immortal after all."

"There are other ways to beat you," Nick lied. He had no idea what he was saying. All he wanted was to make Dark Ness afraid.

"Whatever," she sneered. "We are ten times more powerful than you."

With that, Dark Ness created hundreds of illusions of herself, confusing Nick about which one was the real one.

"Who's the one laughing now?" Dark Ness taunted. Her voice was everywhere, and Nick didn't know which illusion it was coming from.

While Nick was trying to figure out which Dark Ness was the real one, Dark Ruler snuck up behind Nick and trapped both of them in a force field.

"Now, it's time to end you," Dark Ruler said evilly.

"Hey! I was already in the middle of ending him! You can't steal him from me!" Dark Ness whined.

"Finders keepers!" Dark Ruler snapped back.

"Hmph." Dark Ness crossed her arms.

"Anyways, I was saying?" he said, turning back to Nick.

"And we are the immature ones," Nick mumbled.

Dark Ruler created balls of electricity and started shooting them at Nick. Nick tried to dodge, and while doing so, he shot fire from his hands at Dark Ruler."Kayla! You could wake up any time now! Any time!" Nick begged.

No answer.

"Guess I have to do this on my own."

Nick brought out his crossbow and started shooting Dark Ruler. Dark Ruler made a massive ball of light and blasted all the arrows away from him. They went shooting back at Nick.

He tried to dodge them, but too many were coming at him. They pierced his arm, and he fell backward. He plucked the arrow off.

"Oww," Nick moaned. Luckily, his healing quickly kicked in, and he started closing the wound.

"What?!" Dark Ruler yelped. "How is that possible?"

"Oh, did I forget to tell you? I have healing powers," Nick smirked. "Now, let's end this."

Nick turned his whole body on fire. Then, he started to roll around the forcefield border, leaving infernos wherever his body touched. Dark Ruler tried to levitate himself using telekinesis, but Nick unraveled out of a ball and pulled him down from the air.

"What are you doing?" Dark Ruler yelped.

"Beating you."

Dark Ruler stood in the middle of the force field, trapped.

Suddenly, Nick felt a surge of power flow through him. Nothing like he had ever felt before. It repowered his bones, and energy flew through his veins.

"WHAT IS GOING ON?!!" Dark Ruler yelled.

Nick levitated through the air. His eyes had flames in them. The fire surrounded his body, but it didn't look like it was hurting and swallowing him. It looked like the flames were coming from inside of him. The tips of his spiky brown hair turned red and yellow. Instantly, Nick raised his hands in front of him, and all the flames surrounding him gathered together and created a huge fireball. Nick pushed his hands away from each other, and the fireball exploded, going out of the force field. Everything within a one-mile radius exploded. There was a blinding light, and Nick hit the floor a minute later. All the fire disappeared. In the fire, he saw Dark Ruler on the edge of the force field. His eyes were closed, and he was barely breathing.

"Eh, he'll live," Nick shrugged. "I guess he isn't immune to fire like I am."

Slowly, the smoke in the air started to settle. Nick felt all of his energy drain from inside of him. He needed to rest.

"I gotta get out of here," Nick mumbled to himself. "Why don't I try walking out of the force field? Maybe that power surge that I just had would help me walk out!"

He took a deep breath in and charged towards the force field. He winced as he came close to it, feeling like he would slam right into it, but he ran right through.

"Well, that was nice."

He looked around, and a rush of cold air hit him. There was ash and fire everywhere, covering the ground. Some ash was even floating in the air. The sky was as black as obsidian. Nick was still so shocked about what had just happened. *Did I just power up?* He thought. Then, he saw Kayla standing in front of Dark Ness. They were in the middle of a circle of fire. The fire made their faces look red, and they looked powerful.

"When did she wake up?" Nick mumbled to himself. "Why didn't she come when I needed her! Oh well, at least I beat Dark Ruler. But I'm just going to sit out of this one. I want to see how Kayla does against Dark Ness."

He sat on the ground in front of the force field and watched the fight like a movie.

* *

"Hello, Kayla," Dark Ness said with a sneer. "What are you doing here?"

"I'm here 'cause I wanna beat you," Kayla said.

"Well, you can't beat me," Dark Ness said. "I've got a little something called immortality."

"Well, I've got a little something called power and determination," Kayla said. There was a fiery look in her eyes. She concentrated, moved her arm, and lifted Dark Ness off the ground.

Dark Ness struggled. She shot lasers out of her hands, but Kayla moved her hands away from her so that the lasers went somewhere else.

"What are you going to do now, huh?" Kayla asked with a smirk.

"This." Dark Ness duplicated herself, and two of her fell to the ground.

"You've got that too?" Kayla's eyes widened.

"Yep," Dark Ness replied. "And I can control them."

"Fine then," Kayla said. She used her other hand to raise another of the Dark Nesses.

"What are you going to do about the last one?" Dark Ness asked.

"I… um… well, I'm going to fight her then," Kayla said.

"But both of your hands are in use," Dark Ness countered.

"Hands aren't the only things that you can use," Kayla smirked. "I'm going to do something that I have never done before. Let's watch and learn."

She lay down on her back and lifted up her legs and arms. With one leg, she concentrated and tried to lift up Dark Ness' duplication. She rose a little, but then she fell back down. Kayla tried again. Dark Ness' duplication rose a little higher but unfortunately fell back down.

"I sure hope it works this time," Kayla mumbled. "Like people say, the third time's the charm!" Then she paused. "Wait a second, why aren't you attacking me?"

"Um, well, I can't control my duplication unless my hands are free," Dark Ness mumbled.

"What?" Kayla exclaimed. "And you made me do all this work for nothing?!"

"Well, you didn't know that" Dark Ness said. "And I was trying to tire you out so that you wouldn't be able to keep your hold on me, and then you would let me go."

"Well, why did you tell me that?" Kayla wondered. "Well, I'm not going to get tired. And I don't trust you. So, I'm going to put all of you guys in the air and ensure you can't do anything. Then, I'll get a rope, tie y'all up, and drop y'all in a portal. Bam, bam, and bam!"

Kayla closed her eyes and concentrated with all her might. But then, suddenly, Kayla started to rise. All the rocks and ash on the ground began to rise too. Kayla turned into a standing position in the air. Her eyes were still closed, and she had a soft smile on her face like she felt at peace. Her chest was puffed out, and her head leaned back. Her black hair leaned over her back. She started to glow a light golden, and soft turquoise and magenta streaks appeared in her hair.

"Um. what's going on?" Dark Ness asked. "And if she's asleep, shouldn't I be free? This is-"

Suddenly, a large, invisible force burst out of Kayla. The sky turned purple. Dark Ness' duplicates disappeared, and Dark Ness went flying backward into the fire where Dark Ruler was. Since the force was so powerful, she managed to go through the force field and fell right into the fire.

Everything landed back on the ground. Kayla opened her eyes. They turned magenta. She super speeded towards the force field.

"Now, have I beat you?" Kayla asked.

"Yes, yes!" Dark Ness said. Her voice was filled with fear.

"Good!" Kayla yelled. Her eyes turned back to brown.

"Wow," Nick said.

Kayla turned around. His mouth was wide open. She blushed. "Thanks."

"I loved the part where you threw Dark Ness into the force field," Nick said. "So much fun."

"Thanks," Kayla said.

Nick pointed to her hair. "And the streaks? Really cool."

Kayla pulled her hair over her shoulder. "Thanks. And by the way, how did you beat Dark Ruler?"

"Eh, I had a similar explosion like you did. But it was with fire. I got streaks too, see?" He showed her his hair.

"Nice. Where's Ash?"

"Well, let's go find her."

They searched the battlefields. Soon, they found Ash lying down on the floor by Dark King.

"Oh no!" Kayla yelled. "ASH!" She sprinted to her and sat by her side. She checked her pulse.

"Is she alive?" Nick asked.

Kayla nodded. "Yeah. She's just gotten electrocuted."

"Oh, okay," Nick said.

Nick kneeled by her side. "I just remembered that we could heal each other too. I would have done that for you… I just forgot."

"Well, at least I'm still here," Kayla said. "Come on, let's heal her."

Kayla and Nick put their hands on Ash's stomach. A golden glow surrounded Ash. They took their hands off, and the light faded.

"Ash, are you okay?" Nick asked, concerned.

Ash slowly opened her eyes.

"Ash!" Kayla yelled. "You're back!"

"I'm back," Ash said weakly.

Nick and Kayla helped her stand up.

"How did your fights go?" Ash asked. "And Kayla, what happened to your hair?"

They explained what had happened.

"Wow!" Ash exclaimed. "Well, that didn't happen to me. Dark King and I just knocked each other out at the same time. He also took my powers away." Ash created a crystal out of ice. "But he got knocked out, so I guess my powers are back."

"Cool!" Kayla said. "Anyways, we won the battle! Yay!"

"Whoo-hoo!" Nick yelled.

They started to walk back to their ship, jumping and cheering.

But then, they heard a noise.

"Hello, children. I guess you forgot about me," said a familiar voice from behind them.

CHAPTER THIRTY-FOUR:

THE WAR PART III

"What are you doing here?" Ash asked as all three of them turned around to face Dark Star.

"I guess Kayla didn't do such a great job getting rid of me, did she?" Dark Star snarled.

"Hey! I had a lot on my agenda! You can't blame me! And I didn't expect you to get out!"

"Well, anyway, thanks to Ash, I got my powers back. So, now it's time for me to show you what true power looks like."

Nick, Ash, and Kayla formed a line. Nick was in the middle, with Ash on his right and Kayla on his left.

"It's time to par-tay," Nick smirked. He started to charge at Dark Star, but then some force stopped him. He tried to run and push against it, but nothing happened.

"What on Karkarus is going on?" Nick yelled.

"It's a little something I like to call telekinesis," Dark Star replied.

"Thanks for the input," Kayla said. She closed her eyes and tried to grasp the energy that Dark Star was using. She grunted. "I can't grasp it. It keeps slipping out of my hands."

"Well, then it is my turn," Ash replied. She formed icicles and shot them at Dark Star's chest.

Dark Star immediately created a force field with the flick of his hand. "That's all you got?"

"Nope," Nick replied. He moved his hands in circular motions and created a small inferno. He threw the inferno to the ground, and it started getting bigger and bigger. It went towards Dark Star. Dark Star put up his force field, but the inferno went right through.

Dark Star looked shocked. "What on-"

The inferno surrounded him.

"Come on, guys, let's go!" Nick yelled. "He's probably badly injured and unconscious."

Nick created a portal back to their spaceship, and they were about to go back in, but then, suddenly, there was a large explosion behind them. The fire burst away from Dark Star and splattered away in different directions. Then, suddenly, Dark Star appeared in front of them.

"Going somewhere?" he asked.

Nick immediately closed the portal. They couldn't have people going inside their spaceship.

"How did you-" Kayla stammered.

"I am *way* more powerful than you think I am," Dark Star said. "You think that I am just like my children, weak and easily defeated. But no. I am much more powerful than them, and I am *much, much* more powerful than you. You should fear me, but for some reason, you think you can fight me. Well, go on, if you wish. You can try. But remember, there is no-no way you can beat me."

"Fine," Ash said. "Maybe there is no way we can beat you. But that doesn't mean we can't put up a fight." There was pure determination in her eyes.

Suddenly, Ash started to rise. The air turned cold around them, and snow began to fall heavily from the sky. Her chest was puffed out, and her head leaned back. Her hair puffed out in different directions like it was being held by something. She started to glow a light golden, and ice blue and dark purple streaks appeared in her hair.

"What is going on??" Dark Star yelled. "None of my powers are working!!"

"It's something I like to call *a power upgrade*," Kayla said with a smirk.

Suddenly, Ash's eyes snapped open. They were ice blue. Icicles started falling from the sky, hitting everything except Kayla and Nick. The wind blew heavier and heavier.

"What is happening?!" Dark Star yelled, icicles piercing his skin. The wind started to make him lose his grip. He scanned the ground, but there was nothing that could help him hold on.

"NOOOO!!" he yelled as he flew away.

"HA!" Nick yelled. "IN YOUR FACE!" He stuck out his tongue.

"Ah caunth bringth mah togue baack in," Nick said with his tongue stuck out.

"Eh, oh well," Kayla said with a shrug. "It was nice to see you talk while you could. Farewell, my young yet older brother."

"Ah ha-enth daad yeth," Nick said.

"Huh?" Kayla asked.

Suddenly, the wind calmed down. The snow stopped falling, and the wind ceased. Ash's eyes closed, and she gracefully dropped down to the floor. She opened their eyes. They were back to a warm brown.

"Well, that was cool!" Kayla yelled. "You made Dark Star disappear! And by the way, love the hair!"

"Thanks!" Ash said.

"Who said I was gone?" a familiar and evil voice said from behind them. "I've just started."

They turned around. "Where did you come from?"

"About 5 miles away," Dark Star said with a shrug. "I've seen worse."

"Well, now we're ready," Kayla said. "We've all had power upgrades. We're strong enough to fight you, maybe even beat you!"

"I doubt that" Dark Star said.

Dark Star started chasing them with lasers and lightning bolts.

Kayla panicked and quickly lifted up Nick and Ash and super speeded away. Dark Star started to chase them. He was gaining on them and continuing to shoot out lasers and lightning bolts. Kayla continued to dodge every one of them.

"I am coming!" Dark Star said. He was right next to them.

Suddenly, a dozen other Nick, Ash, and Kaylas appeared out of nowhere all around them.

"What on-" Dark Star mumbled. He started to shoot all of the illusions at once.

A dozen more appeared out of nowhere.

Dark Star shot all of them at once.

A hundred more appeared out of nowhere.

"How on Earth is this happening?!" Dark Star wondered. "None of these kids have that power!"

"Wait, what happened?" Kayla yelled. They all looked back. There were 124 of them just roaming around like that, doing the exact same thing that they were. "Who did that?"

"I-I think I did," Nick mumbled weakly. He showed them his hands, which were glowing softly.

"How did you do that?" Ash asked.

"I… don't know," Nick replied.

"Well, you've got a new power!" Kayla exclaimed softly. "Good job!"

"Thanks." Nick blushed.

"I will track your thoughts!" Dark Star said. "The only group that could have thoughts is the real one!"

"Everyone, think about nothing," Nick mumbled to the group.

They all thought about darkness, and they stayed silent.

"Well, where are they?" Dark Star said.

His words echoed in their mind.

"Well, well, well, look who it is," Dark Star said, appearing right in front of them. "Found you."

Kayla tried to turn back, but Dark Star used telekinesis to hold them.

Kayla grunted. She rose Dark Star in the air using telekinesis and shook him back and forth, trying to loosen his concentration. Dark Star struggled against Kayla's telekinesis, and that is all it took. Kayla pushed against the force and shot away from Dark Star. He dropped to the ground and created an enormous tsunami right behind them. Kayla tried running away from it, but it kept following her, going twice as fast as she was.

Kayla stopped. Ash and Nick fell to the floor.

"Kayla, what are you doing?!" Nick yelled. "We are going to die!"

But Kayla just walked towards the tsunami with a dreamy look on her face. She flicked her wrist, and all the water stopped moving toward them. She pushed her hands away from her body, and all the water started going towards Dark Star.

"Whoo-hoo!" Ash and Nick yelled, jumping in the air.

"WHAT ON KARKARUS?!?!?" Dark Star yelled.

"See you later," Kayla said. She turned around. "What was that?!"

"I think you just got another power!" Nick yelled. "I've got illusions, and you've got water! I wonder what Ash will get!"

"Yeah!" Ash exclaimed.

But their victory didn't last very long. The tsunami exploded, and it started to rain.

"Once again, Dark Star is winning," Nick said bitterly.

"Well, we have to keep trying," Kayla said. "We can't just give up."

"I can't believe that Kayla is giving the motivational speech this time, and Nick is complaining," Ash said. "Usually, it is the other way around."

"Hey, I am very motivated," Kayla protested.

"We should get back to fighting," Nick said, interrupting the conversation. "Kayla's right. We can't give up."

"So, let's go," Ash said.

Kayla picked them up and super-speeded them back to Dark Star.

"Not accepting defeat yet?" Dark Star asked. "Don't worry, you will soon. I'll play your little game, but if you guys keep coming, I will have to switch to mind control. And that is not fun."

"Yeah, yeah, whatever," Ash said. "Come on! Charge, do your thing!"

"Oh, I will," Dark Star said.

He raised Kayla into the air. She struggled and tried to push against the force. But nothing happened. Dark Star squeezed his hand. Kayla's eyes widened, and she choked. She tried to breathe, but she could barely.

"What are you doing to her?" Nick yelled.

"Isn't it obvious?" Dark Star said. "Well, anyways, say goodbye to your sister. This is probably the last time you'll see her alive. MWAHAHAHAHAHAHA!"

Ash glared at him with pure anger and growled loudly. Dark vines rose from the ground towards Dark Star. They started to wrap around him.

"What on-" But he couldn't finish that sentence because the vines had already wrapped around him completely.

Kayla dropped to the ground. She took in deep breaths and looked at Ash. "Thank you."

"You're welcome." Ash smiled.

"By the way, you have an awesome power!" Kayla exclaimed. "You can control plants! That is so cool!"

"Thanks," Ash said.

Suddenly, the vines exploded around them, and Dark Star appeared, good as new.

"Well, I'm back." Dark Star smirked. "Miss me?"

Kayla made water appear, and she wrapped it around Dark Star. Ash pulled out vines from the ground and wrapped them around Dark Star's legs and hands, disabling him from moving. Nick created an inferno and put it on Dark Star's head. Kayla rose Dark Star into the air, and finally, Ash shot icicles at Dark Star.

"You know what?" Dark Star said. "I am done playing your little games. Now, it is time for me to show you my real power." Dark Star made a ball of electricity, lasers, water, fire, ice, and a dozen other powers. He moved his hands out in different directions, and the ball exploded.

Kayla, Ash, and Nick froze as the force hit them. The force went on for miles and miles. And then everything went black.

CHAPTER THIRTY-FIVE:

GIVING UP

Nick woke up on the battlefield. He remembered everything that had just happened. Sorrow filled him.

"Guys, wake up," he said.

Ash and Kayla woke up. They slowly recapped everything that happened. Their faces fell.

"We lost," Kayla said. "This is all over. Dark Star will rule the world, and we will just have to sit there and watch because there is nothing we can do."

"How could we have lost that?" Ash exclaimed. "I mean, we got power upgrades and highlights and everything!"

"We were winning until Dark Star showed up. It's just our luck that we did all that for nothing," Nick mumbled from the ground.

"I can't help but feel like this is my fault," Kayla complained.

"Eh," Nick muttered.

"Hey! You should be comforting me! Not blaming me!"

"Well, he was your responsibility."

"Well, you were the one who made the battlefield and the portal. If anything, this is all your fault."

Ash rolled her eyes. "This is all our fault! We just… weren't strong enough."

"Yeah," Nick said. "And we will never be able to be as strong as him. He's had so much practice. The only way we could have won would have been if he didn't have any powers."

"And that isn't going to happen," Kayla said. "Not in a million years."

"Well, we should return to our ship," Ash said. "We can sleep till we die."

"Yeah, there is no point in being awake anymore," Nick said. He created a portal, and they went through. They plopped on their sofa gloomily.

"Oh my god," Willy exclaimed. "What happened? I've never seen sadder people in my life before!"

"WILLY!" They all jumped. "Where did you come from?!"

"I have always been right where you left me," Willy replied. "Now tell me, what happened?"

They explained the battle to him.

"Oh, that's fine," Willy said. "I wasn't expecting you to beat him anyway."

"There's no point anymore," Kayla said. "If we can't beat him, we won't be able to stop him from ruling the world."

"You guys are so lame," Willy said. "Come on, guys! We should be cheering! It's time for us to have a par-tay!"

"Willy," Nick warned, not feeling like joking around.

"I mean it," Willy repeated. "You guys put all of your energy out there. You fought the most powerful villains this universe has ever seen! You beat all of them except one. But who cares? You got power upgrades! You got cool new hair! In all, you guys won."

Ash lifts her head up again. "Really? We lost, Willy. Who cares about hair? We are the worst heroes in the world."

"No, you aren't. You are amazing heroes. You fought Dark Star because you care. You broke into a museum because you care. You did years' worth of research in a few months because you care. Dude, you built a rocket ship and flew to another planet because you care!"

"I get it. We care," Kayla said.

"Willy, what's the point of this pep talk? I mean, we are never fighting again. Forget being heroes," Nick muttered.

"Guys! Enough with lying around! The world needs you right now! Everyone will die without you!"

"Well, then let them die," Ash grumbled.

"I can't believe you guys."

"Well, what do you expect? Kayla yelled. "We lost really severely today. We let the whole world down. But most importantly, we let ourselves down. Unless you have a way, we can beat Dark Star for good. You won't expect anything happy coming out of us.

"Guys, guys, guys," Willy said, shaking his head. "You all forgot the most important thing! The main goal of that battle was to try to beat as many people as possible. And you did. You beat all of them except one. Since you beat nearly all of them, I will now be able to help you make the trap and trap them using that diagram you made. Just tell them to come, I'll make the trap, and BOOM, you win."

"I completely forgot about that," Nick said, standing up. "Okay, here's the plan. We will help Willy send a message to Dark Star using his mind. In the letter, Willy will ask Dark Star and all his children to come at 7:00 am. Since we had already wasted time moping around and woke up around 5 am, we had about an hour and 30 minutes to get ready. We will set up the trap during the remaining time and get ready to destroy Dark Star and his children. Are you guys with me?"

Ash and Kayla got up. The three of them put their hands in a circle.

"Wait for me!" Willy exclaimed. Pulling out a tiny arm from the middle of his body.

All 4 of them put their hands together in a circle.

"On 3," Nick said. "1, 2, 3. GO TECH SUPERHEROES!" They all yelled.

"AND WILLY!" Willy added.

They all laughed. "Sure," Ash said.

CHAPTER THIRTY-SIX:

MAKING THE TRAP

"Now, Willy, I need you to concentrate on Dark Star's face. Imagine his mind and imagine placing this message inside his brain," Ash instructed.

"Okay."

"We thought it over, and we want you to send him this message:

> Hello Dark Star,
>
> Come to our spaceship at seven a.m. today. Bring all your children with you. If you don't come, we will just assume that you are afraid of losing us.
>
> From,
>
> The Tech Superheroes," Kayla said.

"And Willy," Willy added.

"Fine, we'll add your name too. Happy?" Nick grumbled.

"Very," Willy said with a sly smile.

"Let's just get on with this!" Ash exclaimed.

Willy closed his eyes and concentrated on Dark Star. He imagined the message being planted in his brain. When Willy felt a connection, he started to say the letter in his mind.

"Done," he said, opening his eyes.

"Well then," Kayla said. "Let's make this trap."

Nick, Ash, and Kayla all touched Willy and closed their eyes. They sent all the energy that was coming from inside of them into the rock. Ash's powers had a pink aura around them, Kayla's had a blue aura, and Nick's had an orange one. Then, once they thought it was enough, they took their hands off. They put Willy in the center of the trap diagram they had made earlier, and Willy magically started to make it real.

"Yes!" Ash exclaimed. "It worked! And it's awesome!"

The trap had a giant power-absorption machine, another machine that shrunk a person using technology, swung them into a jar and threw them into a net using telekinesis, where they increased in size. There were ice crystals on the floor and lava pits on the sides. Surprisingly, the ice crystals didn't melt, but that was probably because the crystals were made by the rock of creation. Rocks were rolling near them that was supposed to make the object of the trap trip. Four holograms were projected: Kayla, Ash, and Nick, and one of Willy. Near the net was a huge time portal, so the person who fell into the trap would get stuck in a void of time. The best part was that everything was invisible except those who created the trap.

"This is great," Ash said in awe.

"I love it!" Kayla exclaimed. "This is the best trap ever!"

Just then, a blue portal appeared out of nowhere, and a small brown circle plopped out.

"Guys!!" Nick exclaimed. "We just got a letter back!"

Nick knelt down and picked up the small circle. There was a small black button on top, and he pressed it.

A hologram appeared, and it was projecting a letter.

Hello, the so-called Tech Superheroes,

To think I wasn't going to show up.

I will meet you at 7.

From Dark Star

"We now have an evil pen pal, but his letters aren't that evil," Kayla said.

"Kayla now is not the time for jokes!" Ash said. "It is already eleven, and we still have a lot to do."

"He is still our evil pen pal," Kayla muttered under her breath.

"What did you say?" Nick asked.

"Nothing," Kayla mocked.

"Did you just mock me?" Nick asked.

"Yep," Kayla replied with a smirk. "What are you going to do about it?"

"I will make sure you never hear the end of—" Nick started.

"Guys, please stop fighting!" Ash said. "We have to go over the plan! We just have an hour left!"

"Whatever," Kayla grumbled.

"So, the plan is that we will be hidden when Dark Star and his children come in here," Nick said darkly. "I have a hiding spot. When we were making the ship, I hid a secret room in all the important rooms, like this one, an—"

"This is an important room?" Kayla interrupted.

"Just let me finish!" Nick said. "So, if you flip that switch over by the door, a door to the secret room will show up. We will be able to see Dark Star and his children through a monitor, but they won't be able to see us while they are being trapped. Then, when they are put into the jar, we will teleport to that room, ask them all our questions, and then throw them into the time portal. Then, we will bring the rock back to Earth, fix everyone, and actually become The Tech Superheroes! Everyone understand?"

"Yup," Kayla said.

"And by the way, let's try to edit out the part about us losing the battle," Ash said.

"We didn't really lose the battle, you know," Nick said. "We knocked out more people than they did. And the war part of the battle was just the beginning. We've got a lot more coming our way."

Kayla looked at Nick like she was impressed. "Wow, Nick! I didn't know that you could be so wise. We should call you Old Saint Nicholas, 'cause that's what you are. An old saint."

"And that is why I never try to motivate them," Nick mumbled. "Just get humiliated."

"Okay, guys, let's focus!" Ash yelled. "Nick is right. We didn't really lose the battle. I was wrong."

"Whoa, whoa, whoa," Kayla exclaimed. "Is this on tape? Ash just admitted that she doesn't know everything!"

"I know that I don't know everything," Ash said, rolling her eyes.

"Right…" Kayla said uncertainly. "Well, any who, what should we do now?"

"We should tell everyone to stay inside their houses because something dangerous is happening," Nick said. "We must tell them that a guy is trying to destroy the world, so they would likely be safer at home."

"Okay," Kayla and Ash said, then the three left.

Using their powers, the three went to every house and told them about what was happening.

"That went faster than I thought!" Ash exclaimed thirty minutes later as they all entered the room where the trap would be sprung.

"Yeah!" Nick said. "And we still have fourteen minutes left!"

"Wait, fourteen?" Kayla asked.

"How did we get fourteen?" Ash asked.

"Well, we took some time making the plan," Nick explained.

Kayla and Ash each raised an eyebrow.

"Seriously?" Nick put his hands on his hips. "You are going to blame this on me?"

"Well, you did do it!" Ash snapped.

"I didn't waste any time; you guys did! I am the brilliant mastermind who came up with the hidden rooms and everything!"

"Guys! If you keep fighting like this, we will lose more time!" Kayla reminded them.

"Now, how abou—" Ash started.

Just then, they heard a rumbling sound.

"That must be Dark Star! Quick, hide!" Ash and Nick exclaimed as they ran over to the wall where the secret door would appear.

Nick flipped a switch, and a tiny door appeared. He opened it, and crawled into the small space between the walls. It had a creepy vibe, and they couldn't see anything. They were squished, but there was a monitor in front of them.

"What is this for?" Kayla asked Nick.

"I hid cameras around the room where the trap is, and they are connected to this monitor, so we can see what is happening around the room," Nick explained.

"Okay, seriously, when do you do these things?" Ash asked Nick.

"Forget that; let's just see what is going on!" Nick exclaimed.

The large monitor was black and had a small button on the left side of it. Nick pressed the button, and the screen turned on. There were four hidden cameras around the room, each in a corner.

"Okay, we should whisper now," Kayla said.

"Seriously, Nick, if you wanted to hide some cameras, you should have put some in the hallway, so we knew when Dark Star and his kids were coming!" Ash reminded Nick. "And did we even leave the door open?"

"I did that!" Kayla said.

"Okay," Nick said. "But—"

"Guys!" Ash whispered. "They're here."

CHAPTER THIRTY-SEVEN:

THE TRAP

Guys!" Ash shouted. "The trap is beginning."

The cameras allowed them to see everything. The power-absorption machine had just taken away the Darks' powers.

"Good!" Nick exclaimed. "Now, it should work."

"What should work?" Kayla asked.

"The illusions, so we don't have to come out of hiding," Nick explained.

Then the illusions started talking.

"Hello," illusion Kayla said.

"Sit down here," said illusion Ash.

The illusions were right next to the time portal, but Dark Star did not know that.

"Why should we come there?" Dark Star asked. "You come here!"

"Oh, we could," illusion Nick said. "But we have something that we know you want." He held up the illusion of Willy. "The rock of creation. Anyone would want it. But we want to see if you are worthy enough to take it. If you don't come, it means you're weak. Really weak."

"Guys, we forgot about Willy!" Kayla exclaimed.

"I'm right here," Willy said from Ash's pocket.

Kayla sighed in relief. "Good."

"How dare you call us weak!" Dark King shouted from the monitor.

But Dark Star was not paying attention. His eyes lit up, and he started to walk toward the rock.

"Wait, stop!" Dark Chief shouted. "It could be a trap."

"You don't think I would know if it were a trap?" Dark Star roared.

"Sorry," Dark Chief said. "I apologize."

Dark Star started to walk. He didn't feel the ice crystals poking him or anything. He only focused on the rock.

"Uh oh," Ash said. "He's coming pretty fast."

"Well, I'll just teleport us there once they all come," Nick said.

"Yeah, but won't it take away our powers too?" Kayla asked.

"No," Nick said. "This trap has been made to only work on them."

"Good." Kayla sighed in relief.

Dark King followed Dark Star. He didn't feel the icicles either.

"Come with me," Dark Star said. "I would like all of you to have the honor of holding the rock."

Dark Chief, Dark Ruler, and Dark Ness followed. Unlike Dark King and Dark Star, they felt the icicles and realized it was a trap. But they didn't dare to tell their father and eldest brother.

Then, as soon as they approached the shrinking machine, it sucked them up.

"What is happening?" Dark Star asked, coming out of his daze. He tried to use his powers, but they didn't work.

The shrinking device shrank them, put them into the jar, and closed the cap. Then it put the Darks inside an unbreakable net, opened the lid, and unshrunk Dark Star, Dark King, Dark Chief, Dark Ruler, and Dark Ness. Nick opened the portal just then, and Nick, Ash, and Kayla jumped through. They left Willy inside the room because they couldn't risk Dark Star getting it.

"Hello, Dark Star," Nick said. "I see you were fooled."

"You," Dark Star said. He tried to use his powers, but nothing worked.

"What have you done to me?" he howled.

"Fathe-" Dark King tried.

"Be quiet, children!" Dark Star yelled. "Let me handle this on my own."

"We took away your powers," Ash said, ignoring Dark Star's conversation with his children. "Don't worry, it is temporary."

"Why have you called me here?" he asked.

"We are trying to make you good," Kayla said. "What you are doing is wrong. People are dying. And think about it. Don't you think that one person ruling everything isn't fair? Firstly, it would be too hard. Secondly, not fair. Would you like it if one person who wasn't you ruled the world? Lastly, what's the point? What would happen if you ruled the universe? People wouldn't respect you. They'd all be dead. Cause you're killing them. You are only leaving a few alive."

"Now, look." Dark Star laughed. "Do you think I'm going to listen to you, kids? This is my life's decision. I'm not going to let it rest on some little kids like you! I'm over 2 thousand years old, kid." He said it like he was over 50 years old, not 2,000.

"Just because we're young doesn't mean we aren't smart," Ash added. "And if you think about it, you'll see that we're right."

Dark Star thought for a second. "Nope, nothing. Now, will you let me go? I have a world to take over."

"What do we do now?" Ash asked.

Kayla smiled mischievously. “I have a plan. Just follow my lead. Okay, we want to show you what it feels like if we have all the power and you have none,” Kayla said.

“Oh, no, I don’t want to have no power!” Dark Star exclaimed sarcastically.

“Well, how do you think other people would feel then?” Nora asked.

“Well, why does that matter?” Dark Star asked. “It’s not me. It’s them.”

“Well, right now, it’s going to be you,” Nick said, snapping his fingers. Gedlastic 1.0s appeared in their hands. “Not them.”

They took out their Gedlastic 1.0s and started shooting Dark Star with them.

“Ouch!” Dark Star yelped. “Stop hitting me!”

“Fine,” Kayla said, putting her Gedlastic 1.0 down. “Unless you change your mind, we will add very painful elements into these guns and then shoot you with them.”

“Nothing will change my mind.”

Ash shrugged. “Okay.” She snapped her fingers, and small tubes appeared in all of their hands. They pressed a button, and the guns opened. They put the tubes inside, and the gun closed again. They started shooting them.

“Owww! Owww, oww, ow! I haven’t felt pain like that in so long! Not since I was human!”

“You see,” Nick said. “This is what people have to go through. This is what they have to feel. Do you want that?”

“Again, I do not understand why it matters what is happening to them,” Dark Star said. “You know what? I’m done. I am done. I am annoyed with your talk, so I will kill you! Mwahahahahahaha!”

“Look,” Ash told Dark Star. “Do you really want to kill us? Tell me, what will that do?”

"Well, make my life much happier because I won't have to listen to you," Dark Star said.

"Okay, firstly, there is no way for you to kill us," Nick pointed out. "Secondly, you will have to listen to this, whether you like it or not. Thirdly… well, you get the point."

There was silence. "Fine." Dark Star scowled.

"What will happen if you rule, huh?" Kayla asked.

"Well, I will be respected, and people have to listen to what I have to say," Dark Star said.

"But what will that do in the end, huh?" Kayla asked. "You'll get all the glory, you'll rule, but what'll that get you? Nothing. Nothing."

Dark Star thought for a moment. "True. But I will get the glory. That's all I want. Glory. Fame. To rule. And even though you think what I'm doing is wrong, I think it is right. I think that ruling everyone will make everything better."

"But you know what'll happen if you try to save the people instead of fighting them?" Nick asked. "You'll be respected even more. If people think you are good, they may even ask you to rule somewhere. But ruling everyone without their permission isn't going to make things better. It'll just make things worse. And people won't like you? They'll try to fight you and bring you down. You won't get any glory. You won't have any power. People will just disobey you. And I know what you will do. You'll kill all of them, and then who will be there left to rule? No one. Absolutely no one."

Dark Star thought. He continued to think. After a while, he said, "You know what? You're right. All of this is true. If I am good, I will be respected. People will like me. That's all I've really wanted. But I can't just change sides. I've been on the dark side all this time. I can't just change."

"Look, I know you're on the dark side," Ash said. "But if you think about it, darkness is sometimes good. For example, sometimes if you worry, it is good because you can take better care of your family and friends. But at the same time, that is also brightness. Because you are taking care of your family. So, you should never be completely bright or completely dark. A mix of the two is the best combination. But the truth is, having bright emotions will do you better than dark ones. Most dark emotions aren't good. But most bright emotions are good. They make you feel better, and others feel better. Sometimes, it's good to change. But minimally. Not too much. And, if you have a couple hundred or thousand years in prison, and you actually think about it, you might be able to change."

"Yeah," Dark Star said. "I actually believe you."

"So, I mean, like, how do we know if this guy is telling the truth?" Kayla asked.

"Nick, get the mind-reading machine," Ash ordered.

"You don't get to tell me what to do!" Nick snapped.

"Just go!"

Nick created a portal and got the mind-reading machine. He put it on Dark Star, and they looked at the computer. The mind looked like a regular human's mind.

"Wow," Nick, Ash, and Kayla gasped. "So, you have changed sides."

Dark Star nodded. "And now I would like to tell you a secret." He paused. "We are related."

"What?" Nick, Ash, and Kayla exclaimed. "We are?"

"Dark Star nodded. "Your parents' names are June Hall and August Hall. They are my siblings. They lived with me and took the immortality potion, the one that gives powers. But unlike me, they didn't turn to the dark side. You three are nearly immortal; you can't die of old age, but you can die in battle if the injury is bad enough."

Nick, Ash, and Kayla gasped. "We're nearly immortal? That's cool!"

"I have another secret I would like to share," Dark Star said. "You guys have siblings. Three siblings in particular. Your parents asked me not to tell you any more about this yet."

“Whoa, whoa, wait,” Nick interrupted. “Could they be those weird kids we saw trying to get into the museum?”

“You will figure it out soon,” Dark Star said. “You have parents, but you have never met them. They aren’t the people you think they are.”

“Whoa,” Kayla said. “Wait, so who are our current parents?”

“They are your parents’ great, great, great, great, great-grandchildren. Your parents had many children, but then they decided to have more. That was fifteen years ago,” Dark Star said.

“Cool!” Nick exclaimed.

“Now,” Dark Star said. “I have told you everything your parents requested me to tell you. Do you still want to throw my children and me into the time portal?”

Dark Star’s children were silent. They couldn’t think of a word to say. Their father was on the opposite side. They were about to get thrown into a time portal where they would be lost forever. They gave up. They had lost. Finally, they could see some sense. Would they like it if only one person ruled the entire universe? Would they like it if someone was killing them? No. They, too, decided to change sides.

“You can imprison us,” Dark King said. “If we can become kinder and a better person, it’ll be worth it.”

“Yeah,” Dark Ness said. “But make sure you let us out in a thousand years.” She smiled.

“We agree too,” said Dark Chief and Dark Ruler.

Dark Star smiled. “Now go on, Tech Superheroes. Throw us in.”

Nick, Ash, and Kayla felt tears pouring down their cheeks. “Goodbye,” they whispered. “We will let you out. Definitely.”

Nick lowered the net into the time portal, closed it, and it vanished from sight.

CHAPTER THIRTY-EIGHT:

MEETING SHAY

"Why, why, why?" Kayla asked, sobbing. "Why did we throw them into the portal, even though they were good?"

"We had to," Nick said. "It is to make them better people."

"Why didn't we spare Dark Star?" Ash asked, bursting into tears.

"Yeah," Kayla said.

"He needed to explain everything to his children," Nick said. He patted his sisters on the back.

"It is okay, my young compadres," Willy said, suddenly appearing out of nowhere.

"Willy!" they all exclaimed. "Where did you come from?"

"You guys forget that I have powers," Willy said. "Unfortunately, I will not be able to help you much in your next battle against a villain. I shall only be able to fight in battle like you can. But I can only trap the people who helped to make me. And, well, we already beat them."

"It's fine," Nick said. "We'll still take you back to Earth. And…well, maybe you'd like to take on a more… human form after you do your job?"

"Ooooh, yes!" Willy exclaimed. "I want to turn into a boy that is older than you! Maybe ten?"

"Um, we're thirteen," Nick said.

"Oh," Willy said. "Oh. Um, never mind. Maybe fifteen?"

"Sure!" Kayla said. "You can be like the older brother we never had!"

"Um, you have an older brother," Nick said. "Me?!"

"Yeah, but you're not really *older*, older," Kayla said. "You're just a few hours older."

"Um, still older?" Nick said.

"Guys, cut it out!" Ash exclaimed. "We still have to bring Billy back from the hotel!"

"Right," Nick said. "Wait, which hotel did we leave him at? There were so many things going on that I can't remember."

"The Beach Hotel," Kayla reminded him. "Billy loves beaches, so, yeah."

"Okay, cool," Nick said. "Let's get him, and then we can leave."

"I'm pretty sure he's just chillin' at the beach, drinking some lemonade," Kayla said.

"Yup," Ash said. "Chillin' for sure."

Nick rolled his eyes. "We should get going."

"Fine," Kayla said. "But where do we go?"

Nick opened the map. "It's here." He pointed to a big red dot.

The moment Kayla heard that she flew away using telekinesis.

"Come back!" Ash and Nick both shouted in unison.

They chased her down using their ice and fire powers and brought her back.

"Now, you go and get Billy. Nick and I are going to fix the ship and clean."

“Well, why did you bring me down then?” Kayla grumbled. She flew back out and went to the hotel.

* *

Ash and Nick went inside the ship and headed for the engine room. There they took out their tools and started to fix them. Suddenly, a noise came from the control room; it almost sounded like a person.

“What is that sound?” Nick asked Ash.

“I have no idea. Let’s go check it out.”

They ran to the control room and found a girl dancing. She had honey-brown skin, dark brown hair, and hazel eyes.

“Hello!” she said as she kept on dancing.

“Um, what is going on?” Nick asked.

“Aaaahhhh!” Ash screamed.

The girl was dancing like crazy in the middle of the room, shaking her hips, nodding her head, and twisting her toes.

“Okay, how is she doing that?” Ash asked, weirded out.

“No idea!” Nick said, also weirded out.

“Excuse me!” Ash exclaimed, walking up to the crazy person dancing.

“Hi!” she said, turning to face Ash, but she was still dancing.

“Please stop dancing!” Nick said from the doorway. “Also, who are you???”

“Excuse me!” Ash tried to grab her shoulders and stop her, but her hand went right through. “Ahhh! It’s a ghost!” She jumped backward.

“Let me try,” Nick said, walking over and reaching for the dancing girl’s shoulders, but his hand also went through.

“Ahhhhhhhhhhhhhh!!!”

“Okay, who are you?” Ash asked the dancing person.

"My name is Shay Gardener."

"Weird, but okay," Nick agreed.

"Can you please stop dancing and get out of here!" Ash exclaimed. "This is private property, and we have absolutely no idea who you are!"

"Yeah, and obviously, when you are dancing, you need music!" Nick added.

"Right!" Shay said. "Music! Play some music!" Music started playing.

"How did she do that?" Ash asked Nick.

"No idea, but we need to do something about her!"

He went over to the controls and stopped the music. "Okay, first things first. Who are you?"

"I am your computer."

"Seriously?" Ash asked. "You, our computer?"

The computer wore a red leather jacket, white shirt, and blue jeans. She looked like an adult.

"I mean, good choice of clothes, but how are you, our computer?" Ash asked again.

"I was on your parents' artificial planet, but when they came to Earth to visit, they crash-landed," Shay explained. "I was activated with a chip and fell out when part of their ship got damaged. Then someone came by, picked me up, and put me up for sale. Then you guys bought me, thinking I was something I absolutely am not, and now here I am!"

"Wow!" Ash exclaimed. "Cool!"

"What's an artificial planet?" Nick asked.

"Oh, so you aren't that boy," Shay said. "Well, I'll have to explain everything to you then. An artificial planet is similar to a planet but can move around like a spaceship. It can be created using technology."

"Wait, what boy?" Nick asked.

"You'll see," Shay said.

"Cool!" Ash exclaimed.

"Yeah!" Nick agreed. "Wait, remember that time we saw a flying planet? That must be it!"

"Probably," Ash said.

"Where did our parents live?" Nick asked.

"They lived all over the universe," Shay said.

"Interesting," Ash said.

"How did you get here?" Nick asked. "And how do you know what happened to you?"

"When you guys plugged me in, I was still building myself up—" Shay started.

"Wait, building yourself up?" Ash asked.

"Yup!" Shay said. "I was a little damaged when your parents crash-landed, and using a little of your ship's power, I built myself up and came out. I knew what happened to me because once I built myself up, even though I wasn't active, I had a special camera that allowed me to remember everything."

"Okay, makes sense," Nick agreed.

"My turn!" Ash interrupted. "So, we couldn't touch you because you are a hologram, right? And I can't believe I just realized but, parents!!??"

"Yup, your parents knew this would happen, so they gave me a mission I have to accomplish. It includes you and some other kids you will meet later. You guys have to complete the mission. And yeah, that is why you couldn't touch me."

"Sounds weird, but okay," Nick said. "When will we know the mission, and who are these other people?"

"You will find out later," Shay said, then disappeared before Ash and Nick could ask any more questions.

"Well, that was weird," Ash said. "We have to talk about this with Kayla."

"Yeah," Nick agreed. "Now, let's get back to fixing the ship."

"Sure," Ash said.

* *

Kayla walked up to the front desk and turned on her translator. "Hello. I would like to check out Billy Belima."

"Hi," the woman said. "Billy Belima, you said."

"Yup," Kayla said.

"Okay," the woman said. "You can pack his bags and tell him it is check-out time. His room number is 5A. He is currently at the beach."

"Okay," Kayla said slowly. "But don't you do that?"

The woman looked at Kayla strangely. "Why would I?"

"No reason," Kayla said. She pretended to go slowly and then sped up to Billy's room when nobody could see her, quickly packed his bags, and rushed to the beach. There, she saw Billy, lying down on a beach chair with an umbrella over him, snoring so loudly that everyone near him had run away. People watched him nervously and slowly backed away to other parts of the beach. He was wearing a swimsuit, a pair of sunglasses, and slippers. He had a glass of lemonade in his hand, but all the lemonade had spilled.

Kayla giggled. She approached him. "Hello, Billy," she said.

Billy woke up with a jump. "Hello, hello, hello," he said, straightening up. "Who are you?" Billy was half asleep, and he couldn't recognize Kayla through his glasses.

Kayla giggled again. "Hello, it's Kayla."

"Oh, hi, Kayla," Billy said.

"You're totally chillin' at the beach," Kayla said. "Exactly how I pictured you."

"Yeah, cool, whatever," Billy said. "Why'd you come?"

Kayla rolled her eyes. "We told you we'd pick you up once we were done, remember?"

"You're done?" Billy asked. "He's gone?"

"Yeah," Kayla said. She quickly explained what had happened.

"Whoa," Billy said. "That is exactly the opposite of what I thought."

"Yup," Kayla said. "Now, come on! Nick and Ash are waiting for you." She picked up Billy and rushed away.

"Hey!" Billy shouted, then vomited all over the floor.

"Ewwww," Kayla said in disgust.

"Well, don't do that," Billy said.

"Yeah," Nick said. "We've told her a million times."

"Ash, Nick!" Billy shouted. "We won!"

"Yo, Billy," Willy said. "'Sup, I'm Willy."

"Um, hi?" Billy said, confused. "Guys, who on Earth is this?!"

"This is Willy," Ash said. "He's the Rock of Creation."

"Ahh, I see," Billy said. "And… does he normally talk like this?"

"Uh… no," Kayla said. "He's probably just acting like the kids do on Earth. We'll take him there and turn him into a human!"

"Cool," Billy said.

"By the way, your names rhyme!" Ash said. "You guys should be besties once we turn Willy into a human."

"Yeah… I'll pass," Billy said.

"Well, anyway, we have something we need to discuss," Nick informed Kayla. "Come with us."

Nick, Ash, and Kayla all sat in their chairs in the control room as they explained everything to Kayla.

"Okay, wow, that is a lot to process," Kayla said.

"Yeah," Ash agreed.

"And she has a mission for us to work on?" Kayla asked. "And other people are part of it?"

"Yeah, but she will give us the mission later," Nick informed her.

"And when is she going to come out?" Kayla asked.

"Out of where?" Ash asked.

"The controls."

"We honestly don't know," Nick admitted.

"Anyway, we seriously should go!" Billy said from behind them, making them all jump.

"Where'd you come from?" Kayla asked.

"Well, it was taking you too long, but we should leave now anyway!" Billy exclaimed. "We need to go wake up the Earth!"

"Right," Ash said.

Everyone settled in and prepared for take-off. Billy was sitting in the back where they had put a seat. Willy was propped up on the controls stand.

"10...9...8...7...6...5...4...3...2...1!" everyone shouted. The rocket rose into the air and soon out of the atmosphere.

"Let's jump through light speed!" Nick shouted, pressing the button, and they were on their way home.

CHAPTER THIRTY-NINE:

THE END

"Whoa," Ash said after they'd landed. "I'd forgotten how it looked when there were no people." There was no one there. All the plants were dead, and there were no birds in the sky.

They were back at Mission Tech.

"Yeah," Nick said. "But now Billy just has to use Willy and wake everyone up."

"Wait," Billy said. "Why me?"

Nick slapped his forehead. "You have full control over it. More control than us."

"Oh, okay," Billy said. He raised Willy into the air. Suddenly, the trees started to turn green. The flowers and plants began to bloom. Birds awoke from their naps and started to chirp noises in the sky. It was like the Earth had just woken up from a long nap.

"Dude, what's going on?" a random news reporter asked, getting up from the ground.

"Like, IDK," someone replied.

"Why were we on the floor?" someone asked.

People's questions buzzed around like a bee looking for honey.

"Now," Kayla said. "I want to become famous. Hey, you!" She pointed to the news reporter. "Take a video of us!"

The news reporter turned the camera toward them.

"Really, Kayla?" Nick asked.

"Yes! Why not? We deserve some appreciation for what we have done!"

"Yeah, bu-" Nick started.

"Nick," Ash said, putting a hand on his shoulder. "Come on. We do deserve this."

"Fine," he sighed.

The camera turned towards them.

"Hello, everyone," Nick said. "My name is The Teleporter. These are my sisters, The Future, and The Kinesis. Together, we are The Tech Superheroes. We just saved the world today! A minute ago – you guys were sleeping, and you guys were sleeping for three weeks – we were coming back from the planet Karkarus in our spaceship! We went there to fight some villains!"

"Where is your proof?" the newsperson asked.

"Here," Kayla said. She took off the camera that she had put on herself, Ash, and Nick months ago and gave it to the reporter. The reporter skimmed through it.

"Well, it seems like we have some heroes!" the reporter exclaimed.

Everyone cheered.

Kayla puffed out her chest.

Ash also puffed out her chest.

Everyone cheered some more.

"I'm gonna regret this," Nick muttered under his breath, puffing out his chest, too.

Everyone cheered again.

"Who is your leader?" a reporter asked.

"The Teleporter," Ash said, patting him on the back.

"I am awesome!" Nick exclaimed. "I am a leader! And the oldest!"

"Okay, that is enough praise for yourself," Ash muttered. "You just sound weird."

"Fine," Nick said.

"The Tech Superheroes! The Tech Superheroes! The Tech Superheroes!" Everyone cheered.

"Let us pass," Kayla said, and they all passed through the crowd and went into Mission Tech.

Just then, they saw a planet-sized spaceship in the sky above them. Only Nick, Ash, and Kayla saw it, but they thought it was probably nothing.

"Hooray!" Everyone cheered as they walked into Mission Tech. "You saved the day!"

The entire day was filled with festivities, and they all slept soundly that night.

* *

The next few days were filled with celebrations. Every day, there were parties, but nobody knew who The Teleporter, The Future, and The Kinesis were. Only Kayla, Ash, Nick, Willy, and Billy did. People made banners that said, "The Teleporter, The Future, and The Kinesis saved the day!"

Kayla and Ash were very proud of themselves. But Nick thought that it was too much exposure.

"Bad people might come to our town because of this," he told them.

"Who cares?" Ash asked. "We'll fight 'em."

"Yeah," Kayla said. "We're The Tech Superheroes!"

"Fine," Nick said. "But, what are we going to do now?"

"I don't know," Ash said.

"Oh wait, we forgot to turn Willy into a human!" Kayla exclaimed.

"Oh wait, yeah!" Willy exclaimed from Kayla's pocket.

She took him out and laid him down on the floor.

Nick, Ash, Kayla, and Billy channeled their powers toward Willy. Slowly, Willy started to get bigger. And bigger. His gold color started to wear off and turned into a dark olive color. His eyes turned golden brown, and his hair was a curly dark brown. Shorts, a t-shirt, and sneakers formed on him.

He stood up. He looked like a healthy, regular boy. Small biceps were on his arms. He was much taller than Nick.

"How do I look?" Willy asked, his voice sounding the same.

"Look for yourself," Kayla said. She picked up a rock and turned it into a mirror. She showed it to Willy.

"Sweet," Willy said, nodding. "I like being a human. So much easier to talk and move around."

"Guys, what's that?" Ash asked, looking out the window.

They saw a rocket ship coming towards Earth. It quickly landed in the fields of Mission Tech.

"Guys," Ash said. "Who are they?"

They went outside and stood in front of the ship.

People started to come out of the ship. They saw six figures coming out of the rocket.

"Who are you guys?" Nick asked as the strangers turned to face them.

"Finally!" Chase exclaimed, pumping his fist in the air. "Everything worked exactly like it should, Nick, Ash, and Kayla."

"You know us?" Kayla asked. "I mean, yes, we have met, but how do you recognize us through our suits?"

"I will explain later. For now, we have a mission to complete," Chase said.

AUTHOR BIOS

SIYA SHARMA is eleven years old and lives in New Jersey. She loves reading and writing. Every time she read a book; she would wonder how people wrote books – from writing the first line to publishing a finished book. After trying a few different stories, she finally had an idea to write about a game she played with her brother, Rohan and her friend, Sanvi. This story is based on many characters from the game even though the storyline has changed materially after many drafts and edits. She hopes to continue her path towards writing more stories and sharing them with other children.

SANVI JAIN is a young child living in New Jersey. She has always been interested in space, superheroes, and technology and decided, why not make a combination of all three? When Sanvi was younger, she would play a pretend game with her friends, Siya and Rohan about being a superhero and going to space. That game that they played was how they got the idea for this story. Once they were in third grade, they thought, why not just write a book about this?

That is when the process started. Day after day, they would write this book whenever they had time. In the end, after thousands of re-writes and revisions, and tons of new ideas that sprang up in their minds, they finally completed their book. They decided that they would like to share it with the world and open other people's imaginations just like many books opened theirs.